New York Classics, a series devoted to reprinting regional literature of lasting value.

Frank Bergmann, *Series Editor*

At Midnight on the 31st of March. Josephine Young Case

Bert Breen's Barn. Walter D. Edmonds

The Boyds of Black River: A Family Chronicle. Walter D. Edmonds

Canal Town. Samuel Hopkins Adams

The Civil War Stories of Harold Frederic. Harold Frederic; Thomas F. O'Donnell, ed.

The Genesee. Henry W. Clune

Grandfather Stories. Samuel Hopkins Adams

In the Wilderness. Charles Dudley Warner

Man's Courage. Joseph Vogel

The Mohawk. Codman Hislop

Mostly Canallers. Walter D. Edmonds

Rochester on the Genesee. Blake McKelvey

Rome Haul. Walter D. Edmonds

The Traitor and the Spy: Benedict Arnold and John André. James Thomas Flexner

Upstate. Edmund Wilson

A Vanished World. Anne Gertrude Sneller

In the Hands of the Senecas

New York Classics
Frank Bergmann, *Series Editor*

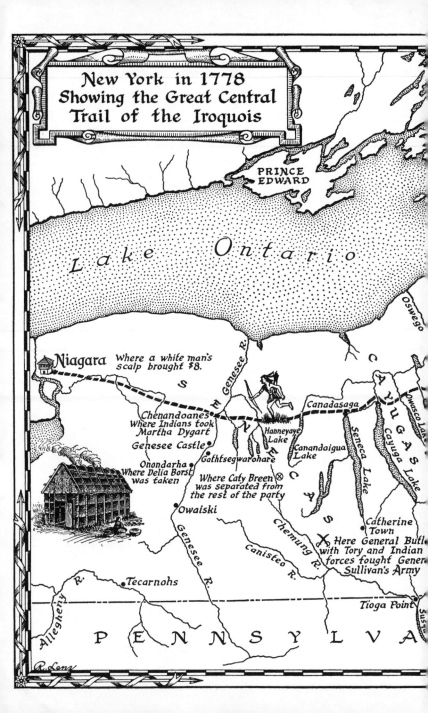

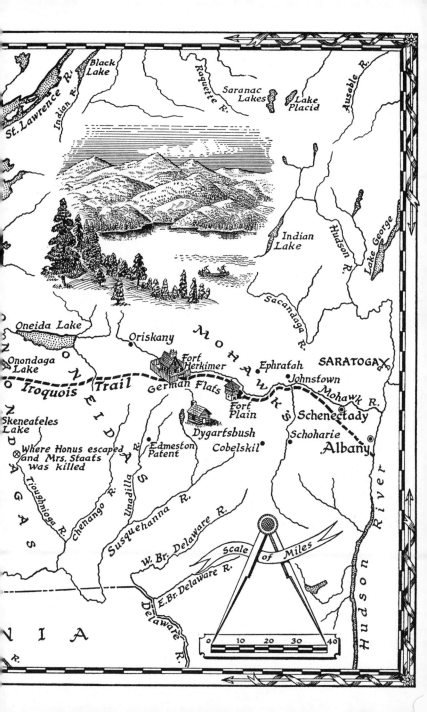

In the
Hands
of the
Senecas

Walter D. Edmonds

Syracuse University Press

First Syracuse University Press Edition 1995

95 96 97 98 99 00   6 5 4 3 2 1

Originally published in 1947. Reprinted by arrangement with
Little, Brown, & Co.

The chapters of this book first appeared as episodes in the *Saturday
Evening Post* (1937). Grateful acknowledgement is made to The Curtis
Publishing Company for permission to publish them in book form.

This book is published with the assistance of the John Ben Snow
Foundation.

The paper used in this publication meets the minimum requirements
of American National Standard for Information Sciences—Perma-
nence of Paper for Printed Library Materials, ANSI Z39.48-1984. ∞™

Library of Congress Cataloging-in-Publication Data

Edmonds, Walter Dumaux, 1903–
    In the hands of the Senecas / by Walter D. Edmonds. — 1st
Syracuse University Press ed.
        p.   cm. — (New York classics)
    ISBN 0-8156-0326-6 (pbk. : alk. paper)
    1. New York (State)—History—Colonial period, ca. 1600–
1775—Fiction.   2. Frontier and pioneer life—New York (State)
—Fiction.   3. Indian captivities—New York (State)—Fiction.
4. Pioneer women—New York (State)—Fiction.   5. Seneca Indians—Fiction.   I. Title.   II. Series.
PS3509.D564I5   1995
813'.52—dc20   95-30617

Manufactured in the United States of America

TO CHARLES STETSON

CONTENTS

Foreword by Frank Bergmann   xiii

The Captives   3

Caty Breen   34

Delia Borst   69

Martha Dygart   103

Ellen Mitchel   133

Dygartsbush   172

FOREWORD

VERY early in his writing careeer, Walter D. Edmonds researched life along upstate New York's canals. *Rome Haul* appeared in 1929, *Erie Water* in 1933, *Mostly Canallers* in 1934. Then Edmonds turned to the War of Independence as it had played out along the Mohawk River. His acknowledged masterpiece, the bestseller *Drums Along the Mohawk,* was published in 1936. Big though it is, this novel did not exhaust all of the material Edmonds had gathered. Part of an early draft of *Drums* saw print in 1949 as *Wilderness Clearing.* Between February and May 1937, the *Saturday Evening Post* published the six stories that were collected in 1947 as *In the Hands of the Senecas.*

Senecas relates to *Drums* in several ways. Like the big novel, it spans the years 1776–1784. The chief character's married name, Borst, is Lana's maiden name in *Drums.* The book gives full treatment to the captivity theme Edmonds had hinted at in *Drums* with Nancy Schuyler and Gahota, the Seneca. Formally, *Senecas* uses the "facet" technique, by which Edmonds refracts the patriotic sentiment of *Drums* into ten sustained episodes. It is a technique that has always seemed to me to express beautifully the emerging nation's Latin motto, *e pluribus unum:* out of essential parts, the writer fashions an organic whole.

In *Senecas,* the Indian raid on Dygartsbush and the trek west toward the Genesee River is a group affair, but once the group is well into Indian territory, it is divided and the parties go their several ways. Edmonds details the different experiences of Caty Breen, who befriends and later marries a captive from another Mohawk Valley settlement; of Delia Borst, who becomes a squaw before she is released following the Treaty of Fort Stanwix; of Martha Dygart, who regains her freedom by killing her mean Indian mistress; and of Ellen Mitchel, who eventually escapes with her fellow captive and future husband Pete Kelly.

The book's conclusion brings us back to a new Dygartsbush after the war. If Edmonds centers on Delia Borst and her husband John, it is because Delia's ordeal as a squaw and her reunion with John are representative of the imperiled as well as the rebuilt lives everywhere along the Mohawk.

Edmond's original title for the book, retained in the first episode, was *The Captives*. It is not as suggestive as the title the publisher substituted, but it is very apt in that it directly connects the book with the captivity narrative genre. The most widely known early example of this genre is *A Narrative of the Captivity and Restoration of Mrs. Mary Rowlandson*. This 1682 account from Massachusetts is marked by a strong Puritan faith, just as the *Jesuit Relations* account of Father Isaac Jogues's martyrdom at the hands of the Mohawks in the 1640s is suffused by Jogues's absolute devotion to his Catholic mission. Delia Borst has no God but only her name to cling to, and the informed reader expects her captivity to evolve into the kind of long life in the lands of the Senecas that is the subject of James Seaver's *A Narrative of the Life of Mary Jemison, the White Woman of the Genesee* (1824).

In *Senecas,* the author's voice is that of an intensely interested observer. His sympathies clearly lie with the captives, but he resists vilifying the Indians. After all, he must first describe life among the Senecas if he is to study its effect on their captives' souls. An Indian reader may find fault and bias; most white readers will readily accept —as Edmond writes in the "Author's Note" to *Drums*— that the writer has "been as faithful to the scene and time and place as study and affection could help" him to be. *In the Hands of the Senecas* is a worthy companion to *Drums Along the Mohawk.*

Frank Bergmann

Utica College of Syracuse University
Utica, New York
May 1995

In the Hands of the Senecas

THE CAPTIVES

DYGARTSBUSH was the last settlement on the west of the Little Lakes District; but there was not a spot in it from which two cabins could be seen at the same time. It was too new for that. Most of the people had come in just before 1776, and their cabins stood in isolated clearings connected only by footpaths to the narrow track that led northeastward twenty miles to Fort Plain.

Altogether there were fifteen families. Though most of them were Scotch-Irish, they had arrived too late to come under the dominance of the Loyalist Johnsons and Butlers. There were also a few Palatine Germans from Schoharie, like Nicholas Dygart from whom the settlement took its name; but most of them were young married couples, like John Borst and his wife, Delia.

Westward the wilderness was unbroken Indian country except for the Edmeston Patent on the Unadilla. But the Edmeston people were king's people, and there was no intercourse between the two places. Dygartsbush was so hidden away that the first year of the war affected it almost not at all. A few of the young men joined the militia; one of the Kelly boys was killed at Oriskany. The Kellys, however, were not the kind of people to be greatly missed in a community. They were perpetually skirting the edge of trouble, either running the woods like Indians with their wild dark faces, or drinking their father into a stupor, or making up to the younger women.

But when the young men returned at the end of the campaign with news of Oriskany and the glorious surrender of Burgoyne at Saratoga, the settlement was so reassured that the people gave up all notion of building a stockade until the spring planting of 1778 should be completed. They did not get word of the early spring raids on Fairfield and Ephratah. They heard nothing of the battle and burning of Cobelskil east of them. There was no possibility of defense therefore, when, on the third of June, Dygartsbush was attacked by over seventy Indians.

The Indians surrounded the clearings individually just before suppertime on the third of June, while most of the men were still hoeing corn in the stump lots. A light spring rain was falling, and under cover of it a few people did manage to break into the woods. Whether these had escaped or been killed, the survivors who were taken prisoner had no way of telling except for the rain-soaked scalps their captors carried at their belts. They could not even tell how many of themselves had been captured, for, as they retired, the Indians divided their band into several parties.

2

The Indians were in a hurry. At the edge of the woods they divided their loot by the light of the burning cabin and made it into bundles for the prisoners to carry. There were only two men in this particular lot, Honus Kelly and his thirteen-year-old brother, Pete. The rest were women, from old Mrs. Staats, the mother of Nicholas Dygart's first wife, down to young Ellen Mitchel. She had been out hunting the Mitchel cow which had strayed nearly to Borst's and had consequently been picked up away from her family.

Every one of them had a load to carry. It took only a few minutes. The cabin burned with a high flame, casting out shadows from the stumps among the corn. The shooting was nearly over — only now and then a single report, followed by the shrill, bursting yell. The old Indian who had taken Delia in the doorway of the cabin half an hour before loaded her with her own blankets, her copper kettle, and her little mirror, that had been her wedding present from her mother. She accepted them dully, standing a little apart from the rest, a straight tall girl, nearly as tall as the old Indian, with a thick brown braid of hair that reached to the joints of her hips.

She had come to Dygartsbush only three weeks ago, having been married, altogether, less than a month. She knew none of the other prisoners well; she felt like a stranger in the community, who still spoke of her as Borst's young bride. Without John she would have felt herself lost, with no church bell anywhere to be heard, no sound but the endless drone of the insects, or the noise of the frogs at night. Even in the daytime the woods pressed against her, unless she could hear the ring of John's axe.

That sound yet thrilled her. Though she might be baking at the stone oven in front of her door and he in the new lot he was clearing, out of sight and a hundred rods away, if she heard his axe she had but to close her eyes, even at noon, and feel the strength of his hands about her, and smell the quick strong masculine smell of his body.

He had gone away the night before to Fort Plain after flour, carrying the grist bag on his shoulder, and she had expected him back for a late supper. She had planned to start it cooking an hour after sunset, guessing the time, for they had no clock, but she had hoped he might be earlier. Her whole being had been tensely alert for the sound of his returning feet.

When she had heard the stick break and had gone to the door, she had seen the head of the Indian in the dim white of the chokecherry bloom on the edge of the stump lot. His little eyes were like small animals, questing here and there to cover the clearing and then fastening upon herself. Even when he stepped out of the brush and raised his hand to his mouth she had not been able to move. But at the first ascending quaver of his yell she had tried to bolt round the cabin.

He came after her, lumbering like a bear with his big stomach, but ugly and swift, catching her by her hair and jerking her back. Then he had finished his yell, his knees bending under him, jerking her head slightly, while two younger Indians ran down the slope from the back of the cabin. The three of them crowded close, so that she could see the shapes of their faces under the paint, and surrounded her with the rank, rain-soaked, greasy smell of their deerskins.

Now the load of the bundle weighted her shoulders. The old Indian, the only one who seemed to have any words of English, said, "You come. Walk fast." He turned into the woods at the head of the line. Another Indian prodded Delia with the barrel of his musket in the soft part of her side, but she hardly felt the pain.

She was remembering John's last words to her. "I'll be back right on time," he had said laughing. "Have a big meal for me, I'll be hungry." She prayed now that he might have been delayed.

As she felt the wet branches on her arms, she realized that the settlement was nearly empty of shooting. She tried to shut out the memory of two screams she had heard from over at Hawyer's. For an instant the new leaves were picked out redly by the light of the burning cabin. Then the darkness overwhelmed everything except the steady padding of the old Indian's moccasined feet in front of her, and the stumbling progress of the women behind.

From way back a new sound broke out, dismal, tentative, wavering in the rain. One of the prisoners behind gave a thin gasp. "What is it?" she asked. "My God." Mrs. Staats's dry old voice answered the woman. "It's the dogs," she said. "They howled like that at German Flats. . . ." Her voice was broken off by a blow. Delia heard her old body floundering in the underbrush, and the grunt of the Indian as he hauled her back into line. She herself suddenly blundered into the leading Indian, who pushed roughly back. "No talk," he said harshly. "No talk any. We kill."

He rapped the head of his tomahawk on his musket butt.

3

Her feet were soaked, and bruised by unseen stones and roots. Her back ached from the load and her legs had become stiff and thick, so that she walked clumsily and found it difficult to regain her balance when she stumbled. She was so tired that the wet of rain began to chill her; her thoughts were wrapped up inside herself; and she was grateful when the march was halted for a prisoner to pick herself up. The Indians made no effort to help; at first they waited silently, but as the delays became more frequent, they used their musket barrels or the flat of their hatchets, beating the prisoner phlegmatically until she could again proceed.

A woman would become panicky at the mere thought of falling. Even Delia, when she came unexpectedly down on her knees in her first fall, struggled up desperately, panting, snatching at the branches with her hands in the effort of getting her feet back under the load. She could hear the old Indian breathing in front of her as he waited and smell his heavy body smell. But when they went on again, and she was not struck, she realized with a sick revulsion that her mind had worked like an animal's, and for a little way her back straightened against her shame at herself. She found that she was silently repeating, "My name is Mrs. John Borst. My name is Mrs. John Borst." It brought the image of her husband close, and she seemed to feel him walking beside her in the darkness, his legs tramping sure and strong, his face kind and solemn with pride of her.

Then the sound of laborious march behind her once more took her back into the line. One woman was murmuring over and over, "Oh my God, oh my poor back, oh he's broke my poor back, oh my God." Delia could not tell who it was from the voice. It was barely audible, droning along at a high pitch, a voice without heart or hope.

A moan followed a blow.

They went on for hours through the dark. None of them had any idea of where the Indians were taking them. None of the women knew the country west of their clearings. Perhaps Honus Kelly could tell by daylight, but he would be the only one.

Twice they crossed shallow brooks, one in an old beaver fly, where the rain sluiced down straight on their bare heads and the Indians herded them closer, and the old Indian in front of Delia spoke again — "Make hurry fast."

She wondered dully why the Indians should feel hurried. There was no one to follow them. There was no one left who might know for weeks what had become of them, or care what had happened to them, unless . . . and suddenly she thought of John.

If he had not reached the eastern edge of the settlement, he might have escaped the raid altogether. There was a chance of that's having happened provided he had been compelled to wait longer than usual at the mill for his turn. Yet even if he had escaped the raid, how would he have found out which party she herself had been taken

with? And suppose he discovered that, he could do nothing **by himself**. He would have to return to Fort Plain for help, **twenty** miles each way, and it was unlikely that the people **there** would take up the pursuit when they must start **three** days behind the Indians. . . .

4

This time the Indians halted them. A few of those behind came up to talk in their own language to the leader. After a moment the latter shouted, "Stop now. Build fire."

The prisoners were brought together in a little group, huddling close instinctively to Honus Kelly, the only man in the party. He tossed his pack off and said, "Give me room," and sat down on a wet log to ease his back.

It was strange to think that before this time, not one woman among them would have had a decent word to say for any Kelly. But now, after a moment's wait to see whether the Indians would resent his having talked, their voices broke out in questions.

"Do you know where we're going?"

"My God," he said, "it's dark."

"What are they going to do with us?"

"I don't know," he said. "Pete, you all right?"

Young Pete Kelly moved up.

"They didn't give me much to tote," he said. Delia could see his face in the first rise of firelight. He was staring at his brother. "They sure loaded you down, though."

For a moment they were all silent, staring at one another.

"Where's Jinny?" Mrs. Empie spoke with sudden shrillness. "Where's my Jinny?" She moved all round the group, a toil-bowed, middle-aged woman. "Who was walking ahead of me all the time?" she said with a fierce accusing note in her voice.

There was a pause.

Presently, a timid voice answered, "It was me, I think."

Mrs. Empie stared. Her face became transformed and violent. "You, Caty Breen! I thought you was Jinny." But suddenly she seemed to lose strength and sat down on the wet earth, leaving the girl she had confronted alone before them all.

Caty Breen was hired help at the Kelly house, a timid, mouse-haired girl, inarticulate, and conscious of the gossip that went round the settlement about the way old man Kelly and the boys misused her.

Mrs. Staats said bitterly, "That little slut."

But Honus turned on her.

"You can shut your dirty mouth. You're no better than Caty is now."

It was the first time anyone had ever spoken that way to Mrs. Staats. The other women looked at her curiously. She glared at Kelly, but bit back her words, and there was a motion of feeling in his favor.

As for Caty, she drew back from their huddled group, her face painfully flushed; and it occurred to Delia that it must have been one of the first good words ever spoken for the girl in the Kelly household.

For a while they stood silently, as if expecting Mrs. Staats to have her say when she had regained breath to say it with, but as she held her tongue the questions began again.

"My man was in the stump lot. I didn't see him."

"They killed Tom," said a woman with a quick rise of voice. "They shot him. I saw one of them stick him with a spear."

Martha Dygart came up to Honus. "Mr. Kelly," she said, "did you hear anything of my two children?"

He looked at her kindly. Martha was a gaunt-faced homely woman, the second wife of Nicholas Dygart, whose first had been Mrs. Staats's daughter. People felt that she did not lead an easy life.

"No," he said, kindly. "I didn't see them. Where was they?"

"They'd gone after the cow. Just before the Indians came. We didn't see them. They killed Nick and Herman but I thought they wouldn't find the children. They'd headed back of your place."

"I didn't see them."

"Mother Staats wanted me to call for them, but I thought they might get away."

Mrs. Staats then spoke. "How'll they get away?" she said viciously. "Two girls, the oldest seven? Martha was scared the Indians would hit her if she hollered to them."

"I was not." The tears rose in Martha's plain eyes. "Before God and Jesus I wasn't, I wanted them to get away."

Honus just stared at her. There was a long silence, which again Mrs. Staats broke.

"Now they'll never get found probably. The Indians killed everybody else."

Delia Borst, for some minutes conscious of rising hysteria, fought to speak calmly. "Did anybody see my husband?"

A small light entered Honus Kelly's eyes as he studied her round chin, the tenseness of her full lips, and the quick color in her cheeks. She looked young and, in spite of her strong figure, still girlish.

"No, why?" he answered for them all.

"He'd gone to Fort Plain," she said. "He went yesterday. He wasn't due back till just about the time."

Honus nodded. "You mean maybe he didn't get back in time to get caught?"

"Killed," said somebody.

"No, no." Delia was not conscious of speaking out loud. But she saw that Honus was studying her, and suddenly he leaned forward to whisper to Mrs. Staats. Mrs. Staats ought to know about such things; she had been in German Flats when Beletre burned the place in '56. "Ask her, Honus," said Mrs. Staats. "She's got grit."

"It would be worth knowing if he was alive, Mrs. Borst," Honus said. "Would you be able to tell his hair?"

"His hair?"

"Yes, ma'am. These Indians has only a few scalps, but I reckon our bunch will meet up with the rest in a couple of days' time. You'd have to look at the scalps."

Delia's eyes blurred. She was conscious of Honus Kelly's eyes still watching her curiously. She gulped down a quick wave of nausea. "I'll look at them," she promised. She felt that John himself would have expected her to look.

"We've got a chance of somebody coming after us if he's alive," Honus said. "John Borst was a smart man."

Mrs. Staats was saying, with a kind of relish, "I'm glad that we haven't got any babies along. The French Indians when they raided German Flats killed all the babies." With her sharp face and dark eyes and white hair dankly straggling down her cheeks, she looked like a witch.

Mrs. Hawyer leaned suddenly against a tree and covered her face, and Martha Dygart turned with triumphant bitterness on the old woman. "That was a thing for you to say!"

"I'm sorry," said Mrs. Staats in her dry voice. "Nobody told me she was."

5

All but two Indians squatted round the huge fire they had built, the flames of which licked up against the rain with a rusty thick smoke and singed the lower branches of the hemlocks. The two Indians came up to Honus, taking him on each side, and threw him suddenly. He made no resistance though he looked big enough to handle them both. They lashed his wrists and ankles to a six-foot pole and left him lying on his back. Then one of them remained as sentry and the second joined the circle round the fire.

They had half a dozen kettles boiling pieces of beef from a cow slaughtered during the raid, and it seemed to the women that the meat could be hardly warmed before they had fished it out again with pieces of bark.

They looked more like queer birds than men, squatting round the fire, with the bedraggled feathers leaning damply over their ears and the braided scalp locks, like some kind of crest or comb, on the crowns of their heads.

Except for the old one who had captured her, Delia found it hard to distinguish between them. He had taken John's best hat, which rode down low on his ears, the brim concealing the upper half of his face. All the others looked young; they had the elaborate unself-consciousness of young men on their first expedition, paying no heed to the soaked group of women standing just outside their circle, and eating leisurely.

When they had finished they motioned to the stewpots, and the women, following Mrs. Staats's example, helped themselves. Having no bark spoons, they tried to fish the meat from the pots with sticks picked off the ground, and the Indians watched with amusement as they blistered their fingers. They did not laugh, but their faces were almost comic with their solemn sense of fun.

It seemed queer to Delia, how the other women settled down to eat. She herself did not feel hungry. All the time she kept looking at the scalps hanging from the Indians' belt thongs.

She had never seen a scalp before, and again and again she had to force her eyes back to them in an effort to judge the color of the hair. Where it was long she had no trouble, knowing it for a woman's. But those with shorter hair did not show up their color plainly by firelight.

To her they had a limp tattered look like rags left hanging in the rain, until with a shock she recognized Nicholas Dygart's by the bald piece fringed with grey, and before she could help herself, she turned to Martha Dygart.

Martha saw her, looked, saw the scalp, and stopped chewing suddenly; as suddenly she rose and disappeared among the trees. The old Indian spoke in his own language. The man to whom Martha belonged got up, drawing out his tomahawk, and followed her. The rest, while they listened to Martha, could see his impassive figure on the fringe of firelight a little way off from her. He stayed there till she came back into the light and sat down against a tree.

Trembling, Delia continued her search. Though it was no longer possible for her to avoid seeing the scalps as parts of human bodies, she felt a growing hope. She ought to know John's, she knew she could tell it if it were there. She began to move around the Indians, and they, all at once, understanding what she was after, with the same half-amused glances lifted up the scalps, some even with an air of pride, like peddlers showing calico, turning the hair for her to see.

The last scalp had fine yellow hair. She knew it for a child's, the little Bowen boy's. She had often come upon him hunting imaginary bears with the wooden guns he made of sticks.

Tears rose to her eyes.

"Don't cry, ma'am."

Startled, she looked down and found that she had walked near to Honus Kelly.

He was looking up at her from his stiff position on the ground. "You going to eat that meat?" he asked.

She found that she had come away with her piece in her hand. "No. You haven't had any food, have you?"

"No," he said. "I could stand some food before they load me up tomorrow." His eyes made her feel ashamed for not thinking of him before. "You'll have to hold it for me, Mrs. Borst, if you don't mind."

She sat down beside him and held the meat to his mouth. It was a clumsy business, for the beef was fresh and tough. She had hardly strength to hold it against the wrenching of his teeth. But it comforted her oddly to be helping him. If John had been caught, he would be tied the same way, she thought.

"I saw you looking," he said, after a time.

"Yes."

"It weren't there?"

"No."

"I'll bet he did get off," he said.

She looked at him earnestly. Of all the talk she had heard about the Kellys, their drunken old father, and the boys running wild in the settlement, no one had told her they were kind.

"Don't you want to get back with them women?" he asked, when he had finished. "You've fed me fine."

"No." She looked down on his greasy mouth and impulsively knelt and wiped it with the hem of her petticoat. He lay quietly, staring at her.

"You don't mind?" she asked him.

"No. Thanks. I was wondering how I'd get it done."

"What happened at your place?"

"I guess they got the boys," he said. "Pa was in his bunk

and they kilt him there. Drunk and asleep. He never knew it. I was fetching in the wood for Caty." He met her eye and colored slightly. "Caty's a good girl," he said. "You look out for her, won't you, ma'am?"

"Yes, if I can. What do you mean?"

He did not answer.

"What are they going to do with us?" she asked after a while.

He thought it over. "They can do different things. They're Senecas, and I can't understand but a little of their talk. I know Oneida better. I think they come from a little town called Onondarha. I don't know where it is."

"Yes," she said after another pause.

"They get eight dollars for a scalp at Niagara," he said. "They get more for some men prisoners and less for most women, they think. They's been some talk whether I'll fetch eight dollars." He chuckled. "I won't."

"Oh," she said. "Do they know that?"

"The old bugger that took you, his name's Gasotena; it means High-Grass; he's telling my bugger I won't. They'd save food scalping me. But my bugger don't believe it. He's saving for a muskit and wants to find out about me at Tioga. 'Pears Colonel John Butler's down there." He heaved his shoulders. "Ma'am, I got to get away afore we get to Tioga."

She said, "Oh," helplessly again.

"I'll have to have some help," he said.

"I'll help if you'll tell me how."

"Thanks, but I don't know yet. Pete ought to help some.

Pete's making friends with them, him and that little Mitchel girl, Ellen. See."

The two children were sitting among the Indians, and the girl was staring with wide eyes at the painting on the naked chest of the Indian beside her. He seemed a little pleased and turned ostentatiously to let the firelight shine on the place.

To Delia he looked as simple as the children.

"He took both the kids," said Honus. "Name's Skanasunk — means Fox. He's real pleased with himself."

"What'll they do with us women?" asked Delia after a time.

"I guess some of you'll get took to the villages. They'll keep you there to work, maybe. They may sell some of you. It's hard to tell. Old High-Grass there's been talking about you."

"Do you know what he says?"

Honus shifted his eyes.

"I couldn't make out. Maybe I'll know later."

"Will you tell me?"

"Oh sure, sure."

She said, "If John got away, I've been wishing he could know I was alive. I don't think he could come after me now, do you?"

His eyes came back to hers and he said soberly, "I don't think he could, ma'am. I hate to say so."

"I wouldn't be afraid if John knew I was alive." She hesitated. "If you could get away, would you tell him that for me?"

"I surely would." His face was dead in earnest. But he

was obviously disinclined for further talk. He had closed his eyes.

Delia kept still at his side. She would not care what happened, if only John could be informed. She felt a kind of faith in Kelly. She knew rascality was in his blood, however kind he was to her, and surely he would think of some way of escaping. Let him think. She tried impotently to steer Mrs. Staats away with her eyes. But the old woman was white with anger.

"Honus Kelly," she said. "Just look at where your brother's got that little girl. Right in among those naked savages!"

Kelly rolled his eyes at her.

"What do you tell me for?"

"Tell him to come over here."

"Do you think the little rat cares what I say?"

"Well, make him mind."

"I can't. Try yourself if you like."

"I did. He said for me to hunt a hen coop."

Honus laughed out loud.

At the sound of his voice the Indians surrounded the prisoners and began binding their hands and ankles. They were then left to settle themselves. Mrs. Staats found it hard to get comfortable.

"Look at those children now," she said.

Delia looked. The boy and girl had been allowed to remain at the fire, and their bodies now lay between those of the blanketed Indians.

"Her Ma would die if she saw Ellen with a Kelly," whispered Mrs. Staats.

Delia lay down on the wet leaves, and shut her ears to the bitter old voice. The rain providentially had stopped; there was only the drip from the trees, a sound barely heard through the hiss of the burning logs. As they sank into coals, the darkness came closer and the hemlock trees assumed infinity. The prone figures of Indians and captives, even the two watching Indians crouched down inside their blankets, were small enough in the wilderness to bring the barred owl close. He passed over them with a silent ruffle of his feathers, turning on one wing when he reached the upward fire's warmth.

6

The weather changed with their marching. Even the nights grew warm, and the lack of rain was a godsend to the older women. There was an element of timelessness in their march. The woods looked all alike to them, and even the old Indian, High-Grass, nosing from one deer trail to another, had the air of a careful dog finding his way through strange country.

The Indians were in no hurry, now, and as long as their captives kept moving at all, they left them alone. At night Honus was the only person they thought fit to bind. It was fortunate for the women, as they were tormented by the flies. They seemed like bait, drawing the insects from the Indians; except for the few cool hours after the dew had settled, it was almost impossible to sleep.

The Indians had washed off their war paint, emerging as rather harmless-looking brown men. They were uniformly darker-skinned than the Indians Delia had seen in the Mohawk Valley. They did not, however, relax their watchfulness; and she felt that underneath their apparent indolence there was the same impersonal aptitude for cruelty. Only the two youngsters, who were allowed to come and go as they pleased around the nightly camps, attained any familiarity with them.

The two began to assume a manner of superiority towards the other prisoners, Pete Kelly more than the girl. On the day that the Indians stayed in camp while a party of them hunted, Pete borrowed a line and fishhook from Skanasunk and went off down a brook after trout, taking Ellen with him.

Delia sought out Honus, telling him. "Do you think he'll get away?"

Honus said, "No, he won't try to. Peter's clever. He knows that they're watching him."

It was as Honus said. That evening Pete and the girl returned with a string of trout which they turned over to Skanasunk. The Indian manifested a faintly pleased surprise and the children acted up to his manner, as if neither party knew that the Indian had lain up in the woods all day watching them. But to Delia, Skanasunk's behavior was the first really human action she had observed in an Indian. . . .

The next evening, just after sunset, they heard a human voice in the woods. And shortly after, another party of Indians joined them. They had only three prisoners. But instead of joining the women, who were exchanging their experiences with a passionately tragic zest, Delia began another search of the scalps carried by the new party.

By now the Indians had had time to dry and mount them on hoops, in the Indian fashion, and they showed their sex and color plainly. But the Indians were holding a council and made it plain that they did not want her around. She was compelled to move away, sitting by herself and watching their motionless figures.

They did not talk like white people. All but one kept silence, while he had his complete say. She tried to make out from their faces what they were thinking, and she kept looking at High-Grass, who, though the oldest, waited for the rest to be done.

Long before he opened his mouth to speak, darkness had come, and Pete, who with Ellen had been replenishing the Indians' fire, came up to her.

"Honus wants to talk with you," he said in his offhand voice. He did not look in her face, but stood with his head turned, his lean slight figure erect.

"I been looking for you," he continued unexpectedly. "John Borst ain't with them."

"How can you tell?" she whispered.

"I know what he looks like," Pete said. His voice was contemptuous. "Honus told me to look. But these buggers that have just come, they say they chased a white man, a big man, they said, clear back to Otsquago Crick. They said he dropped a bag of gristing. I guess that was him all right. Weren't no other man after grist that day," he added suddenly.

"How do you know, Pete?"

"Crimus," he said. "I know what happens, don't I?"

He swung away from her abruptly.

7

Until nightfall, now, the Indians tied Honus without poles, fastening him to a tree by cords around his waist. He was sitting so when Delia approached, his back drawn tight to the tree trunk and his big body thrust forward against the cords. "It ain't so bad," he said, "once I can work up some slack."

Delia could not hold back her news.

"By Jesus," said Honus. "He's a queer little cuss, ain't he? He never told me that."

His eyes kept steadily on hers, and she wondered why, until he said, "We mustn't talk too loud. Pete thinks one of them new Indians knows English." Delia felt her hands turn cold. He saw the quick excitement in her face and nodded, leaning towards his hands and grinning to himself. "I been waiting for this time," he said.

"Tonight?" She thought, Why now, with all these new Indians watching, too.

He nodded again. "I know what you think. I figure these Injuns will figure the same way. But there's something else. Pete took a knife to clean them fish with. It ain't been missed yet. I got it in my pants. Will you set down?"

"What do you want me to do?" she whispered.

"Don't whisper. Talk low, but so anyone can see you're talking. Their heads is chuck-full of money and the jinks they'll have when they get home. You got that knife all right? Good girl. Hide it in your dress. When they throw me tonight it would fall out. You'll sleep close by and pass it over?"

"I will." She could not help her whispering now.

He grinned at her, a wide grin, showing his big stained teeth through his beard.

"Keep your pecker up. Hain't nothing to get rattled over. Just move around natural and easy and ask Mrs. Staats and Caty will they come and see me. Caty first."

Delia obeyed. She hunted up Caty and said that Honus wished to talk to her. The girl started to her feet, her face changing from white to red, looked once in Delia's face to make sure she wasn't being fooled, and crossed the camp.

Delia saw them sitting side by side, Caty with her hands in her lap and looking straight away from him. The girl sat like someone entranced, a slow blush coming and going in her face. Honus too kept looking at his hands. But he appeared to be speaking earnestly for him. When he was through, she looked at him an instant, rose, and stood irresolutely before resuming her former place. Then she sat staring across at Honus, only turning her eyes when he raised his.

Delia waited awhile before moving on to Mrs. Staats and announcing that Honus wished to speak to her. The old woman had got back a lot of dander from the one day's rest.

"Honus Kelly! Wants to speak to me? Why don't he come over here?"

"How can he?" Delia said. "I'd go if I were you, Mrs. Staats."

Mrs. Staats stared coldly up at her.

"Hurrrmph! I guess I'll go after all."

She got up jerkily and made her way over to Kelly. Delia, thinking she had better show an interest in someone else, found the child, Ellen Mitchel, for once away from the Indians.

"Hello, Ellen," she said. "It must have been fun fishing."

"It was all right. That pig Pete wouldn't let me have the line hardly at all though. Said I was too clumsy."

She still had the lanky figure of a girl, only the small points of her breasts hinting the change she was hovering near. She was all brown, a pretty brown, thought Delia, brown eyes, brown hair; she would be a pretty woman in her time, with her full red sulky underlip.

"He won't talk to me now," Ellen went on, "and the Indians chased me away." Then her eyes grew large with interest. "Have you seen what they did to the scalps? Skanasunk's been painting his. He doesn't do it very well though."

"Doesn't he?" asked Delia, absently.

"I don't think so."

8

Honus Kelly looked at Mrs. Staats's foot where the sole of her shoe was parting from the upper and her bare toe showed through. He didn't give her a chance to speak her mind.

"Set down," he said. "We ain't got much time for talk."

She was too surprised to refuse. She had never expected a Kelly to order her about.

"You've never had much use for me, Mrs. Staats. But I ain't thought much of you either. You've done a lot of damage in the settlement with your talk. Take Caty. She ain't had hardly a friend since I hired her to cook. You knew they was lies. And you've done the same with other people."

Mrs. Staats stiffened. "Well," she said icily.

"I'm not trying just to get you mad. I know you think you having more money than anybody else makes you better than us. Maybe it does. I don't believe you earned any of it though — no more than I ever earned, I bet. But you've got more nerve than all the rest of these women put together. That's why I want to talk to you."

"Me, nerve!" the old woman ejaculated.

"Yes." He grinned at her, looking almost friendly. "I've always said to Pa you were the dangedest old bitch turkey. That's why I want to ask you something. I'm going to get away from here tonight. But I can't manage it alone."

"And you think I'd help, hey?"

"Yes, ma'am."

"You do? Why?"

"When this business ends, you'll want someone to know where you've been took to, if the Indians don't hand you in to Niagara."

"Oh, really. It's nice of you to think of me."

He grinned again. "I'm the only man in this bunch of heifers," he said. "I don't want to run the gantlet."

Mrs. Staats looked down at the hard-veined hands in her soiled petticoat.

"What do you want me to do?"

"I want you to have some bowel trouble," Honus said. "After the logs break down in the fire. There's been only one Injun watching."

Mrs. Staats looked sharply up. "That all?"

"Yes," said Honus.

Suddenly she smiled. To Honus she looked very much like a leering madam in a trappers' house he had been to in Albany once.

"Give me three minutes, ma'am."

"Oh, more than that. The trouble I've had," said Mrs. Staats. Her face was almost pert.

9

Delia lay close to Honus. Ever since the fire had started giving out, her hands had been like ice. She wondered whether she would ever outgrow that trick — she'd been that way from childhood, and whenever she most needed her hands they became clumsy.

Honus's big shape bulked between her and the fire. The Indians had poled him, and she knew that she would have to cut him free. His chest swelled and sank with a regular heavy snore.

The Indians slept, like logs of wood laid out under their blankets. Only the one who watched sat upright, his head like a bare gourd balanced on his shoulders, and his thin face watching the coals.

The top log fell with a brief burst of sparks and a licking of flame along its shattered length. As if the noise had made him restless, Kelly heaved over in his sleep. His snoring caught, broke, and regained its rhythm. She could not see his face, close as it was to hers, but on the bubble ending of a breath he said, "Keep your pecker up." Another breath. "Where's Pete?"

"Sleeping with the Indians just like always."

"Keep your eye on Mrs. Staats."

A breath. "You'll have to saw my hands free. Can you get the knife out?" His snores went on.

She moved with infinite precision, inch by inch, fishing the knife out of her breast and feeling a slight sting as its edge marked a vertical line. Kelly's snoring went on undisturbed. She could feel his breath come and go against her face. She began to fumble for his hands, finding the cords. The knife cut slowly.

"Oh," she whispered, feeling the wet in her fingers.

"Hush up," he said. And the next breath, "Go ahead, damn you."

She could feel how tense his hands were, and then as she went to work, out of the tail of her eye she saw Mrs. Staats lean up on her elbow, heard her moan. The Indian's head cocked like a buck deer's.

"Quick," said Honus.

Delia, all at once, bore down with all her strength. She felt a fresher flow of blood from his wrist. Then his huge paw jumped away and took the knife out of her hand. He twisted down and cut the ankle cords with two quick slashes.

It made a little sound and the Indian swung towards them. But Honus was lying stiffly again with his breath coming and going like the strokes of a stump mortar.

Mrs. Staats, mumbling to herself, was walking quietly away. The Indian moved after her phlegmatically.

The silence settled down. They could hear only the faintest rustling where Mrs. Staats was, but suddenly Honus grunted under his breath. Delia could not hear what he said, something about an old bitch turkey. And the Indian stepped out of the circle of firelight.

"Good girl," said Honus. "I'll tell John Borst. Good luck."

10

It happened like the springing of a deer. In an instant Honus was on his feet, a towering shape over Delia; then in a single leap he had cleared the firelight and she heard his feet on the damp ground and the thresh of underbrush. The watcher's musket exploded and his feet started after Honus. There was a wild screech from beside the Indian, and a desperate scuffling.

"Go on, Honus. I've got him!"

Mrs. Staats's voice, vociferous, triumphant, rose in the night. It was only then that Delia saw the Indians springing up around their fire. Half a dozen of the youngest milled for an instant, before the watcher came blundering back, dragging the old woman by one arm. He pointed the direction Honus took, dropped Mrs. Staats, and led the way furiously into the woods.

The other Indians leaped on the women, knocking them back to the ground and binding them. Even the two youngsters were bound, the girl whimpering a little over the tightness of the cords. But Pete looked over at Ellen and winked his eye, like a lewd small replica of Honus.

They waited all night without sleep. Again and again Delia thought she heard returning footsteps; but they never came till dawn. But then she had to take only one look at the Indians to see that Honus had escaped.

II

Mrs. Staats died during the night. She made no complaints. She lay with the gash in her head and her broken shoulder, staring at the leaves above her face. Once she pronounced Delia's name. But she got no further, or if she did her voice was too faint to carry from the spot where the Indians left her. Her scalp was taken by the Indian who had captured her just before the return of Kelly's pursuers.

Next morning, early, the Indians took up their march. They were hard on the prisoners now, dealing out frequent blows. Honus's load was shared between half a dozen, giving them all they could stagger under.

They dodged the Tioga towns, passing straight west across the southern edge of the Cayuga lands.

The women no longer had anyone to tell them where they were going, for Pete ignored them. He took pains to avoid them once the Indians had restored him to his former favored place.

But six days later, just after dawn, a couple of the Indians dropped out from the trail where it crossed a hill and headed north. They took Caty Breen. Delia said good-bye. But Caty, understanding that she was to go a different way, could hardly speak.

It was while the other women were looking after Caty that Pete edged up to Delia.

"They're splitting up," he murmured. "Me and Ellen is going with Skanasunk. Going to adopt us, he says. You're going on with the main bunch. Old High-Grass figures he's going to make a squaw of you."

The boy looked just like Honus, slightly malicious, altogether wild, as he added, "Honus knew, but he didn't have the guts to tell you."

Then he moved away.

Delia stood still staring after him. She had acquired an

apathy from the long days of marching, and her body sagged from her load.

Then, surprisingly, as the old Indian poked her forward with his gun, her head came up.

Honus had got away. By now, perhaps, John would know she was alive. Nothing but that mattered.

CATY BREEN

For the women Honus's escape meant a renewal of the harsh treatment the Indians had used at the beginning of the march. Loaded down with the pitiful plunder of their backwoods cabins and wearied out with eighteen days of plodding through the woods, stung by the flies and the constant urging of the Indians' hickory gads, their minds dulled and their courage nearly spent, they scarcely took notice of the dividing up of the war party near the head-waters of the Chemung River. Two Indian braves had taken Caty Breen to one side of the main trail and then, as the others passed on, led her away northwards along a path as narrow and overgrown as a fox's alley.

2

Once she looked back; but the trees, multiplying behind her and moving together, had shut off her view of the other captives, and she realized that she was alone, following the two Indian braves to their town. She did not know the name of it; she had no knowledge of the Indian language even if she had dared ask a question. She did not know that already she had come nearly two hundred miles from Dygartsbush. She did not think of the journey by miles, but by days, and she had lost track of time. Except once when the party had lain in camp to let the

Indians hunt, one day was like another: the morning effort to raise the pack, when her body was stiff and lame from lying all night on the ground without a blanket; the endless plodding behind the Indians' feet, over rough ground, with the rain on her head, or still worse the sun and heat bringing out swarms of flies that trailed the winding march in clouds. Her body had acquired a habit of walking bent under the load of her pack, and her eyes ached from watching the slow progress backward of the earth beneath her feet. The dull complaints of the older women filled her head.

She herself had been too shy to talk of her own suffering. She knew the other women did not like her but now, as the green summer woods closed over her, she missed their querulous utterances. The hushed episodic voices of the noonday birds, the click of grasshoppers springing from the grass — these sounds surrounded but were not for her.

The trail led steadily northward, following a shallow valley through upland country. The two Indians moved at an easy pace. They walked as if the land were familiar to them, without taking notice of landmarks. They paid no attention to the captive. She kept watch of their backs for the least sign that they noticed her. Now and then she could hear them talking to each other in their sonorous voices, higher pitched than a white man's, and each time she wondered if they were discussing her, and wished desperately that she might understand enough to know what they wanted of her. All her life she had tried to please people so that they would not hurt her.

Neither of them carried anything beyond his personal equipment, his old French trade musket, powderhorn, bullet pouch, blanket, skinning knife, tomahawk, and the little medicine bag on his chest.

The dark coppery brown of their skins was smooth and worked over their shoulder blades with an almost liquid freedom. The sun glistened on the oiled planes of their backs as they moved. The braided scalp locks on the crowns of their heads were like bird crests; they made motions with their heads like birds when they looked to one side.

She remembered suddenly what Honus Kelly had said to her: "Don't ever show them you're scared."

They had come to a stream, a wide brook with swift water, which the trail crossed at the head of a long run. As the Indians waded through, she saw that the water came over the top of their leggings and knew therefore that it would reach well above her own knees. The water was roiled, as though there had been a black storm back in the hills. She felt surprised for they had had no rain for several days along their line of march and she stopped beside the edge and speculated vaguely about it, unaware of the time she was taking as her eyes were caught by the run of water.

Her shoes had long since worn out; she was barefoot. Her legs and feet showed the dried scars of briars and a trickle of blood passed over her right ankle and ran to earth beside the instep. During the march she had learned to fix her hair in two braids hanging down in front of her like an Indian woman's to keep it out of the way of the pack. Its soft brown, drawn smooth from a wide part to show the round of her head, and the drooping corners of her mouth were more like a child's than a woman's.

She heard the Indians shout above the rush of water, and she looked up with quick fear. Her forehead wrinkled a little under the tug of the burden strap. The Indians' eyes seemed to reflect the sunlight, not to take it in as white people's did.

One of them beckoned. She tried to nod, but the burden strap held her head immovable. She stepped into the water, felt the current take hold of her petticoat, then thrust against her knees. The pebble bottom rolled under her feet. Overweighed by the bulky pack, she floundered, stopped, and struggled for balance. Looking up again timidly she saw the two Indians still impassively watching her with muskets cradled in their arms. "Don't ever show them you're scared." They were always angered when a a captive fell; they would not want their plunder wet. Her own good blue shortgown was in the pack, but she no longer thought of it as hers. Sweat drenched her face and shoulders as she felt her way, one foot after the other, and finally reached the far side. She felt them looking down at her and she had to take hold of the bank at their feet to pull herself up. Her glance came level with the hooped scalp of old man Kelly whom they had killed in his bed, the grey hair almost long enough to be a woman's.

Their eyes were like hawks', bright and expressionless, above the broad hard cheekbones, and she stood submissively within a foot of their bare hairless chests, smelling their faintly sweet smell of grease. They looked away, swung onto the trail one behind the other without a word.

3

They had covered over twenty miles and late in the afternoon she noticed that the Indians were watching the angles of the sun. They had been going since sunrise, not stopping to eat at noon like white people, but chewing bits of their pressed food as they walked. They had given her a bit, tasting of maple but smelling so strong of the Indian smell that she covertly let it drop from her mouth. Her neck and the muscles across her shoulders were sore from her burden and there were long stretches when she seemed to be walking in sleep.

The first narrow trail they had taken had turned into a second, the second into a third, each seeming more traveled than the last. Now the third entered still another, a well-beaten path, that dipped downward sharply to a lake and followed its margin under tall timber. There was little underbrush here, and she could see out between the straight boles of the trees to the water. It stretched north and south, unruffled, clear and glassy.

The two Indians talked to each other, pointing at the sun and at trees along the bank. Again and again she thought she heard the same word repeated, *Hanneyaye,* as if it might be the name of the lake. Whenever the Indians uttered it, their voices seemed to rise. Then, after four more miles of traveling, a sound like barking dogs carried over the still water from the north. Almost at the same moment, the Indians swung from the trail, mounted a knoll, and began questing among the trees. They moved forward steadily until a deep exclamation from one brought them together. Caty, sagging tiredly beside another tree, saw him point to a deep blaze.

One of them pulled out his tomahawk and made a new blaze under the first while the other squatted down and, taking a small sack from his belt, began mixing paints.

Not knowing what they were doing or how long they would stay, Caty dared not remove her pack. She knew nothing about the ways of Indians except the stories she had heard from the Kellys or trappers visiting their cabin. These had had mostly to do with deals in pelts. They came crowding back into her brain, distorted even beyond their original telling. "Don't ever show them you're scared," Honus Kelly had said to her. She felt herself begin to shake and, to keep erect, leaned her shoulder against a tree.

The Indian with the paints began making marks on the tree; but she could not have told what they were except that they looked like the drawings a child would make. His companion, resting on his musket, watched over the other's shoulder. Once in a while he pointed a finger and said a word. When the painter had finished, they contemplated the work together: two men carrying guns, these could be recognized. One prisoner on the line below, shown by the pack. A circle with rays depending from a horizontal line — it looked like the sun, but meant to them a scalp taken. The solemnity of the two Indians was immense as they surveyed the record. They were young men; it was their first expedition; they brought a scalp, a prisoner, and plunder. There was eight dollars apiece in it for them and they felt that they were rising in the world.

Then the one who carried old man Kelly's scalp laid it down, together with his musket and blanket, and trotted away down the other side of the knoll. The second Indian, to whom Caty belonged, set his musket down also and sat down upon the ground and began to mix his own paints. Feeling Caty's eyes upon him, he said something to her. She started at his voice; her eyes had been watching without registering what they saw. She took a tentative hesitant step towards him and stopped, sudden color rising to her pale cheeks. She felt dizzy and put her hands up to grasp the burden strap beside her ears.

The Indian imitated her motion and, carrying it farther, gestured that she should put the pack down. She stared a moment, only half realizing. Then, seeing him absorbed in his work, she eased the strap from her forehead and let the pack fall behind her. The release from its weight sent the blood rushing to her head. Her ears roared and she leaned forward, started to fall, and barely caught herself with her hands. She felt the pack at the small of her back and leaned gratefully against it, until the roaring ceased and her head partially cleared. "Don't ever show them you're scared."

The Indian looked up from his work. The sunlight was almost level in the trees. The Indian's face meeting the light was cut in hills and valleys; the eyes were shadowed by the cheekbones, and the arch of the nose and the slope of the forehead picked out. The redness of his skin was accented, and the braided lock cast a shadow over the left side of his head. She saw the slight flutter of his nostrils as he regarded her. Beyond him to the north, the barking of dogs was suddenly clamorous, shrill and unmistakable.

The Indian stopped his work to lift his head. She too heard the voice of the other Indian. At first it was so high in pitch that she was not sure it was human. But after a moment the rhythm of the Indian speech became clear; and it was as though she heard the Indian talking ahead of her on the trail, only that he had gone a great distance ahead.

When the voice died the clamor of dogs was renewed, and for a while she listened to it, dying away, bursting suddenly forth again and fading. Finally it ceased entirely, and the woods were still.

In a little while the second Indian returned to sit down beside the one who had stayed and began mixing more of his own paint. He came so quietly that she was hardly aware of him until he had settled. They were wholly preoccupied in what they were doing and she forgot to think of them and let her head lie back against the pack. The water of the lake deepened and slowly took fire from the setting sun. A flock of pigeons, like a drift of colored smoke, passed from the far shore, their wings making a whisper overhead. Out of sight, down the lake, a bittern started his hammering cry and stopped abruptly. The sunlight passed from her ankles beyond her swollen feet. She raised her eyes furtively to the Indians.

She bit her lips to check the cry in her throat. Gravely and with laborious care, they had painted their faces. The black and white war paint had turned them into masks under which the features were distorted and in an instant the quick horror of the raid that had been dulled by the long days of travel returned to her. She saw again the sudden appearance of the Indians beyond the corn-piece fence; the boys running for their guns; Honus felled by a glancing tomahawk in the doorway of the cabin. She heard old Kelly's one drunken roar and the shrill cries the Indians made running over the corn and the shooting breaking out through the settlement.

But the Indians were absorbed in their preparations. Satisfied with the effect of their paint, which they examined in turn in a piece of mirror, they took turns in rebraiding each other's scalp locks. They had scarcely finished when they heard people approaching along the shore of the lake. They rose silently, taking positions behind trees.

Caty also heard the approaching footfalls. Looking down towards the water she saw two Indian women carrying bundles in their hands. Neither looked up toward the knoll.

The two squaws set down the bundles and retreated. As soon as they were gone, the braves went down to the path, picked up the bundles, and stepped off into the woods. For minutes on end Caty sat alone in the fading light. "Don't ever show them you're scared." There was no one to see her now. The tears came unchecked to her eyes and rolled out upon her cheeks. She huddled down beside her pack, drawing a small comfort from its familiarity.

Then she heard the Indians returning. They were dressed in fresh clothes. Even in the waning light the beading on the leggings and the quill work in the moccasins shone faintly white and red and yellow. Their heads were covered with bright cloths mounted on hoops, from which the eagle feather slanted backward, and over their chests the crossed shoulder belts were pinned with silver brooches.

They picked up the muskets that Caty had never thought of and gave her their blankets to add to her pack, showing her what to do with motions of their hands. She was stupid in understanding and when she finally did, her hands shook so that she could hardly force them under the binding cords. A sense of their impatience made her fingers clumsy.

She knelt with her back to the pack, drawing the burden strap to her forehead. The coarse bark webbing pressed against her forehead as though the fibres found their former imprint there; the weight dragged against her neck; and she drew her breath with a gasp and struggled upward. The Indian prodded her with his musket, sending her forward.

Within half a mile the path stepped down into a deep worn slot running east and west. She did not know that this was the great central trail of the Iroquois but its hard-beaten earth was smooth under her feet.

Even so she stumbled. Nearly thirty miles of travel in a day under the pack had taken all her strength. Her mind seemed to have risen from her body, dissociating itself from her exhaustion, and like a night bird, silent overhead, it followed her and the two Indians eastward into the dusk.

She seemed to hear the clamor of the dogs far below and see the glow of fires from the house doors. The houses, built of logs or bark, narrow and long, were scattered between apple trees, and the inhabitants thronged toward the edge of the town, preceded by a low-running mass of dogs. She could see the two Indians in their fanciful fresh clothes, the kilts swinging over their knees and the feathers nodding on their heads, and herself, bent over, stumbling in their wake. The Indians moved as if they had no knowledge of her presence. They looked straight ahead into the town, between two lines formed by the squaws and children, to a central fire burning before the council house and a bare post stuck in the ground beside it. Beside the post a solitary Indian stood, erect and old.

As the dogs lanced out along the trail, the two braves lifted their knees high and their voices pierced her ears, over the barking of the dogs. The dogs were all around them now; one snapped at the hem of her raveled petticoat and another clicked his jaws on her scarred ankle. The flash of pain brought back her mind, like sickness entering her body. She was aware of making motions at the sharp, foxlike heads of the dogs with their lolling tongues. Just before her the two Indians stamped their heels, a step at a time. She heard a dog yelp, as clubs rained down on them; she was in the midst of the Indians, smelling them rankly, and it seemed to her swimming thoughts as if each last one of them were yelling.

The women struck at her and the children poked sticks

at her unsteady feet. The instinct to run came over her; but she was hemmed in and the two young braves, dancing their slow dance, would not let her through the bedlam until the heat of the central fire struck her eyes. She looked up to see them driving their tomahawks into the post. Then, in the midst of silence, the old man waiting there began to speak and she stood wavering, behind her captors, while his voice rose and fell.

It came to her ears like the voice of a preacher; at times it was almost gentle; at times it lifted as if with exhortation. A prayer came into her head, but she could not say it.

The old man ended his speech at last. The Indians gave a shout. As the silence swept in from the surrounding night, Caty was seized by the women. She felt their hard brown hands on her arms; the pack was yanked off her shoulders; and she was dragged out of the circle. Behind her one war whoop was echoed by the crowd; even the women dragging her yelled. Their eyes gleamed as they turned their heads backward towards the fire. Their faces had not the impassiveness of the men's, and Caty shrank as she saw their hatred of herself.

The war whoop was succeeded by a single voice singing a war song. It was a kind of chant accompanied by a drum, given with high, rapid utterance. She could hear it still going on as she was pushed through the door of a narrow cabin. She stumbled forward into pitch blackness, tried to get her bearings, and sat down without a sound on the dirt floor.

Beyond the log walls, the singer's voice went on to a wild climax. The beat of the drum was heard for a moment by itself; then the war whoop was repeated. She tried to shut it out, huddling on the earth and holding her head in her hands. "Don't ever show them you're scared." There was no one to see her now. She wept silently as the voices faded and a brief moment of still-ness, like an owl's wing, passed into the cabin, pene-trating her consciousness with almost physical pain.

Then, all at once, she rose on her knees and listened. She had not been mistaken. Somewhere in the dark of the cabin she heard another person's breathing.

4

"Who are you?" It was a man's voice.

She said, "Caty Breen."

After a moment she asked, "What did you say, mister?"

The man cursed. "Why do they have to keep on holler-ing and yelling like that? Why can't they shut the door? My God, I'm sick of it."

"It isn't as loud as it was," said Caty. "I mean, it doesn't seem so loud to me."

"They've just gone into the council house, that's all. They'll keep it up all night, I know." His voice was hoarse. Because it also sounded muffled, she thought he must be lying on his face. When he wasn't speaking, she thought his breathing seemed heavier than was natural. She could hear it, if she listened for it, even over the yell-ing of the Indians.

But it comforted her to know that she was not the only

white person in the town. She sank back on her heels as she knelt, clasping her hands in her lap.

Suddenly the man asked, "Did they treat you bad?"

"Not awful bad, I guess," she replied. "They made me carry a pack and we walked a long way today. I didn't have any shoes. But they didn't whip me the way they did some of the other women." She paused. "Not until we got here. Then some of the women hit me with sticks."

He said, "I guess it ain't bad if you ain't a man," with bitterness and self-pity. She heard him draw his breath, and his voice sounded stronger as he asked her where she came from.

"Dygartsbush," she said simply.

"I never heard of that place," he said. "Where is it?"

"It's a settlement over in the Little Lakes country."

"I never heard of it," he repeated obstinately; but then he added, "But I never been south of the Valley."

"Where did you live?" she asked. She was too shy to ask for his name.

"I settled in Kingsland, me and my brother and his wife. Near Snydersbush," he said. "They raided there this spring, but we'd moved into Little Falls. I went back to the farm two weeks ago. No, it was longer than that. What's to-day?"

"I don't know."

"God," he said, "don't you know what day it is?"

"I'm sorry."

He asked, "Where are you? I can't see."

"Here."

"Can't you come closer?"

"Yes," she said, "if you want me to."

She crept forward on her knees, feeling for him with her hands so that she would not stumble over him. He was lying on a kind of low platform. She touched his bare arm. He put his hand out and groped for hers. He seemed to have spells of difficulty in his talking. "My name's Henry Shoe. I was well regarded in Snydersbush." He withdrew his hand and said, "Oh, God damn them Indians"; and then as the yelling was followed again by the drumbeats and the single singing voice, "I had to go back to our place. They told me I was a fool, but I had to. I couldn't get out of my mind my corn piece didn't have no scarecrow there to scare the crows with and nobody living there, see?" His voice rose. "I didn't even get the thing set up when a bunch of them come at me. They got me. I couldn't get away. The God-damned painted devils."

Caty was silent so long that he roused himself.

"Maybe you think I was a fool, too?"

"No, I don't," said Caty.

"Maybe you don't like how I talk. I forget and get cussing."

"I don't mind cussing," she said.

"I reckon you're a nice girl though," he said, and was silent himself. Caty even thought he must be sleeping, when suddenly he said, "It's nice having someone to talk to. Kind of takes your mind off what's outside. You awful tired?"

"Oh, no. I couldn't sleep."

He asked, "Did they do a lot of damage at your place?"

"They burnt the whole settlement," she said. "They killed all the men but Honus Kelly and Pete, his brother. He's really only a boy. And we thought maybe Mr. Borst had got away."

"I mean *your* place," he said fretfully. "They killed your family?"

"I haven't any family," she said. "I was hired girl to Kellys!" She added a moment later, "I've been hired out to people ever since I can remember."

"These Kellys now — was they nice people?"

"There was old Mr. Kelly, and then Honus and Tom and Frank, and Joe and Pete were all his sons. People in the settlement didn't like them much. You see," she went on anxiously, "it was just they didn't do much work. They drank a lot too, especially Mr. Kelly. He was drunk when the Indians come and Honus said he couldn't have known what happened to him." Her voice dropped. "The women in the settlement didn't like me working for them. They said a girl couldn't be decent living alone with them. They wouldn't speak to me, not even after the Indians caught us. But the boys weren't bad, though they were always scaring me. They kept fighting. They let the corn go all to weeds and I tended the garden piece myself. But they were dandy hunters. They made some money trapping and trading pelts with Indians."

"I've seen that kind of man." There was scorn in his voice. "They just rant around the woods as bad as Indians theirselves."

"Kellys just wasn't working people, I expect," she admitted. "I was scared there, but I didn't have no other place to go. They laughed at me the time I asked to go back to Fort Plain, and there wasn't no work in the settlement for me anyway. I tried once. But they weren't bad men. They didn't trouble me. I told some people that, but they didn't believe it."

"I don't believe it," said Shoe. "It's the women talk like that."

"I know," she said, "but once in a while the men would try to talk to me" — she felt herself flush in the dark — "when I was berrying. Honus caught young Rob Hawyer at it once and gave him a terrible trimming and then he talked to me about how a girl should act."

"Yes," said Shoe, but his interest had changed. "How old are you?"

"Eighteen," she said.

"It's awful dark in here," he observed. Then, as if he recollected something, "But a fire would bring in the flies."

"I like it better dark," she said.

She could hardly hold her head up. Suddenly she realized that the noise from the council house was fading out. She turned her head towards the door, seeing the dim glow from the central fire and the figure of a watching Indian and a couple of dogs in front of it. The Indian faced the prisoners' lodge.

Henry Shoe shifted himself on the platform.

"I thought I would go crazy," he said. "It's wonderful having a person to talk to. I been in these lodges all along at different towns and heard them hollering. You get more scared when you're alone."

"I know," said Caty, softly.

It **was** some time before she realized that he had dropped off to sleep. His hand, hanging over the edge of the platform, lay against her arm. She was careful not to wake him; and she moved only enough to stretch out where she was on the dirt floor. His fingers trailed along her arm until they rested on her shoulder. She let them stay, drawing a sense of friendliness and comradeship from their touch.

5

The light of sunrise, finding its sole entry through the door, fell first on her. She woke uncertainly, lying still at first to listen to the wakening birds, and letting her eyes move round the cabin.

It was windowless; the log walls were solid from end to end. There was no fireplace or chimney. Fires had been built upon the floor, and the smoke, allowed to escape through small vents along the rooftree, had blackened the rafters, making a faint bitter scent of creosote. Down each side ran two platforms, the lower about a foot above the ground, with the upper five feet above it. There was no other furniture, nor any bedding. It seemed to Caty more like a stable than a place for people to live in.

As she stirred and sat up her shoulder brushed the hand of her fellow prisoner. She turned quickly to look at him.

He was a big strong fellow, but she thought that he seemed very young. He lay like a boy, flat on his belly, with his head turned to pillow his cheek on his hand, but she saw at once that his sleep was not a boy's, but an utter, drugged surrender to exhaustion. Then, as the light gained strength, she understood why he did not lie on his back.

One glance at his tattered hunting shirt, the welts and open gashes showing through the rents, and the cloth stuck tight to the clotted blood, told her what he would have to go through when he woke. Her heart turned sick with pity, and she thought, if only she had some heated water she could ease his pain by soaking off the rotten cloth.

She moved softly to the door of the cabin and looked out into the village. Smoke was already rising from the chimneys or roofs of a few houses, but some of the Indian women evidently preferred to do their cooking out of doors. Caty saw one of them fetching two kettles up from the brook. As far as she could see none of the men had come out; there was only the brave left to guard the prisoners, sitting under his blanket a little way from the door, and the dogs that slunk back and forth with anxious steps and nosed towards the cooking.

Caty watched the squaw hang the two kettles on a cross stick over the flames and turn aside to speak to another woman who was coming out of the woods with a faggot of sticks on her back. Their voices were slow and unconcerned as the morning utterances of birds. The town lay peacefully among the apple trees; the long narrow houses looked low on the ground, with their elm-bark roofs grey in the green leaves. It was a clear, warm morning; a blue sky, without clouds; the smoke rose untroubled by any wind.

After the woman with the wood had gone her way, the one who had set her kettles over the fire turned into her cabin. Perhaps it was the peacefulness, perhaps it was her deeply ingrained instinct to serve people that gave Caty courage to do what she would never have dared for herself. She stepped from the door and walked directly to the fire. She paused there for an instant; but there was no sound from the near-by house. Her heart fluttered as she lifted the cross stick and slipped the bale of the nearest kettle over the end. Hurrying back to the prisoner's lodge she met the watching Indian's eyes. And she stopped, trembling, a little way from him.

But his unblinking stare had no expression. He was like a coiled snake under his blanket with his opaque small eyes and beveled head. "Don't ever show them you're scared." She had a brief thought of Honus Kelly, then, and stepped past the Indian. She expected at any moment to feel his hand. But he did not stir, and in a moment more she was inside her cabin.

6

She heard Shoe groan.

"Don't move," she called softly to him and hurried forward, setting the kettle down beside him with a shy triumph that he never saw. But he did see the kettle and understood what she wanted to do, gratefully.

She tore a piece of calico from her shortgown to make a wad and moistened it.

"I'm afraid it'll hurt you," she said, "but it won't be so bad as if I didn't soak it off."

She began at the lower part, working up towards his shoulders. He winced from time to time, and she said, "I'm sorry. I can't help it. I'm going as easy as I can."

"Where'd you get the kettle?"

"I found it on a fire," she said. He mustn't fret, she thought, and she lied. "They let me take it."

He didn't say anything to that; he didn't speak at all but lay with his face on his forearms and bit his wrist.

"Poor boy," she said, as she finished, and blushed vividly, realizing what she had said. But her heart swelled. She had never done anything like this for anyone before. It was not like cooking for a man or fixing his shirt, in which you were just hired help in the house. It was a different thing altogether. And he seemed not to have minded being called "poor boy" either. Let the squaw come after her kettle if she wanted to. The shirt was free.

Shoe groaned as he moved to draw the shirt over his head and Caty said, "I wish I had some salve to put on it; but I'd like to wash off all the cuts anyway."

"It feels all right this way."

"It ought to be done, I think." She hesitated. "There's two places where it's festering."

"Leave them alone." He started to roll over. But Caty touched his shoulder with her hand. Her fingers looked calloused and brown against his white skin. Suddenly she pushed the shoulder down, gently and firmly saying, "Please let me fix it. It would be better."

He gave way sulkily. She could not see his face, but she felt a queer stirring in herself as it occurred to her that she had never before told a person what he must do. Now she had tried to, and Shoe had given way. Her small face, with the heightened color in the cheeks, and the large grey eyes absorbed in what she was doing, became tender.

"It must have been terrible," she said quietly. "What did they do to you?"

His voice was muffled.

"I had to run the gantlet." She felt the muscles tighten under her hand.

"I'm nearly through," she said. "Did you have to do it here?"

"No, it was the town before we got to this one. I don't know what it's called. It's a big place on a big lake. There was almost two hundred of them lined up."

Caty said nothing, but he went on talking just the same, in a thickened voice that was almost desperate with his effort to make her see how it had been.

"Squaws and children and the men too. They had clubs and hickory sticks and knives. It was yesterday morning and I hadn't had a thing to eat. Nothing." He twisted his head round to look at her, and the sight of her mild face with its soft brown braids framing the cheeks seemed to rouse his dislike. He went on bitterly, "You're just a girl. You don't know what it was like. They say they don't make women run it, generally. Standing you out there alone at the end. I was the only prisoner they had. There wasn't anybody with me only the two Indians that caught me back in Snydersbush. One of them could talk some English. He told me to run through them lines and touch the post in the middle of the town. He told me to run fast. But I was scared. I said I didn't want to."

"It must have been terrible," Caty repeated. It was all she could think of to say. She wished she could think of something that would soothe him. But he acted like a feverish man. He looked a little feverish, she thought.

"When he told me to go, I couldn't move. I couldn't, honest. I was scared, but I couldn't move. The Indian said if I ran fast I wouldn't get bad hurt. But I didn't believe him. You couldn't believe him, seeing them — with knives some of them. They was wicked." He swallowed noisily. "Then they took me by the arms and dragged me to the line and pushed me, but I couldn't help it. I hung back on them. And then one hit me on the shoulder with his tomahawk. It's sore there now but it hurt awful then. I couldn't hardly see. But I tried to run then. I run as fast as I could but I felt sick with being hit on the shoulder. And a God-damned little girl stuck a stick between my legs and I fell down. I thought they'd kill me before I could get up. I couldn't see at all then. I couldn't even think, the way they was hollering and yelling and laughing some of them, too, the bloody-minded dirty devils . . ."

He broke off suddenly and put his face on his arms.

"Don't do that," Caty said. "Honest, you mustn't. You mustn't show them you're scared. I've got your back fixed now, pretty well."

She set aside the kettle with its bloodied water.

"Thanks," he said, "it feels some better." He sat up and put his feet on the floor and looked her full in the face. "Ain't you scared of them, too?"

His face was just beginning to lose the boyhood roundness; it had a yellow fuzzy beard. She wondered how old he might be.

"You ain't seen what they can do." His underlip thrust out a little. Looking back at him, she wished he was a little older, or less afraid so he could tell her 'what she should do. Then she thought of his back and what he had gone through, and she felt ashamed. It came over her suddenly that that had come only from the gantlet. She remembered a description one of the Kellys' trapper friends had given one night, of a bunch of Cayuga Indians burning a hostile Indian to death. This trapper had looked on with a bestial curiosity, it seemed to her, not to miss a single trick.

She felt again in her breast the premonitory stirrings she had felt before. She must not let Henry Shoe think of the way they tortured prisoners to death; but it was as if her thoughts had entered his.

"They burn some men," he said. His lips worked together and he tried to manage a dispassionate tone of voice that to Caty sounded pitiful.

"They say some men, strong ones, can live three hours in it. Maybe more. I'm powerful and strong-bodied. I can carry two hundred pounds of grist. I carried it once five miles home. My brother Len he couldn't do that. And he's three years older than me. They don't only burn them . . ."

"Hush," said Caty. "It ain't good to get scared before a thing begins to happen."

"God, don't you *think*, too?"

"I try to think of all the things I want if I had a place of my own. That helps. There's so many things." She smiled at him. When she smiled her mouth had a way of bending sharply at the corners that was quite lovely.

"They burned my place," he said.

She said, "I wonder hów we get anything to eat."

"Oh, they'll bring in a mess of something. They did at the other town. Where you going? You ain't going out, are you?"

"I'm going to take the kettle back. She may want it."

"So she didn't let you take it," he said triumphantly. "You just stole it."

Caty lowered her eyes before his.

"Well, I did."

"I reckon she'll act mean. They're meaner than weasels, some of them women. You better not go out."

Caty hesitated. Then it came to her that if she went out, and showed him she was not afraid, maybe he would conquer his own fear. His struggle with it was so plain in his face. He hadn't the gift to hide things. He wasn't like the Kellys. He had been brought up decent and hard-working, to work a farm, not to get captured by Indians.

But he had worked on her own fear, and she turned her back on him lest he see her face.

The woman whose kettle she had was arguing loudly with a couple of others, pointing to the stick over the fire and the solitary kettle there. The watching brave had got up under his blanket and walked over towards them, as if to listen. Caty lifted her head and walked out of the cabin.

They saw her instantly. The squaw to whom the kettle belonged came up to her with blazing eyes, snatching the kettle with one hand and striking Caty across the face with her free hand. Caty felt the blood on her lips; and instantly the other two squaws rushed up. All three were yelling at her; but Caty tried to smile. "I had to have water," she said. She had to speak to keep her lips from shaking.

Her voice seemed only to rouse them further. They put out their hands at her and the one with the kettle swung it suddenly. Caty could not have dodged if the brave had not taken her quickly by the arm and drawn her back away from them.

He spoke to the women and then turned Caty round towards the cabin.

"Stay inside," he said. "Bring meat soon."

He walked behind her to the door and thrust her in.

7

Henry Shoe sat where he had when she went out. But he looked at her curiously.

"I heard them hollering at you," he said. "Did they hurt you?"

Caty shook her head.

"They must've. I heard them. They hit you on the mouth.

I can see though the light's back of you." He stared out through the door past her. "God damn them all."

Caty wiped her lips with her bare arm.

"No, no. It ain't bad. Honest. One of the men brought me away."

"Did he tell you anything?" Shoe asked eagerly.

"He said we'd get food pretty soon."

"I could eat it now. I'm hungry enough to eat it if it was a dog. Raw dog."

Caty felt herself go sick.

"Oh!" she whispered. "Do they give you that?"

"I've heard so. Listen. Did he tell you anything else? About me, I mean. What they're going to do with me? I'd like to know."

She shook her head.

"God," he said. "I'd like to know."

He wouldn't though. The sweat on his face showed her that.

"Don't think of that," she said.

"How can I help thinking of it?" he cried and turned himself away from her.

She sat down miserably, wiping her mouth from time to time and rubbing her arms clean on her petticoat.

Outside they listened to the growing of the Indians' day. They could see the Indians passing back and forth before the door — women fetching wood and water, children passing back and forth; the men standing in groups of two or three, doing nothing, except one man who brought in the carcass of a doe; and the everlasting dogs.

Neither of them spoke until, an hour or so later, a

woman brought them a small bark dish of stew. Then Henry relented enough to say to her, "It ain't dog anyway. Have some?"

She felt so grateful that he had noticed her again that she could hardly speak. Even as they ate she felt his mounting nervousness. He was like an animal, the way his head kept rising to each fresh note of sound, each passage of a body across the door.

He got up finally and began walking up and down the open space between the platforms and she saw then how big he really was — a great heavy powerful fellow, nearly six feet tall.

Now and then he would retail what was going on outside. He was tense; his voice sometimes rose in inconsistent irritation. It was some time before he noticed how quiet she had become.

"Say, Caty, you ain't mad at me, are you?"

"No."

"Honest?"

"Honest," she said.

"I'd hate for you to feel mad at me." He sounded pathetically anxious. "You been nice to me. I don't think I ever met a nicer girl than you."

She raised her eyes.

"I'm glad, Henry."

His eyes were simple and honest. She saw once more how decent he really was. It wasn't his fault he was decent.

Then, like a wave of light, it came to Caty what the feeling in her breast had been about. She understood that he depended on her not for the work she could do for him, but for herself. Herself who had been a hired girl all her life, who had always been so timorous of other people. They were both white people, the only white people among all these Indians. She saw that that was why he must not act afraid, no matter what.

In the inexplicable workings of providence, she, Caty Breen, who never in all her life had had a moment of actual pride, now experienced the pride of blood and race. She could not put it into words, even in her own mind; but her small face was made radiant.

A sort of peacefulness came between them that had nothing to do with the steady noises of the Indian village, or the warm clear sun beyond the door, or the blue sky. The man sat down again and quite easily began to talk to her about the farm he and his brother had started. He told her about the color of their cow and when she should have calved; of the sugar bush they had and the brook that would run a mill — it had a ten-foot fall, so that they would hardly need a dam, and the body of water in it was steady, summer and winter. He told her about his sister-in-law, a steady girl, but not a first-rate cook.

"I'll bet you're a good cook," he said.

And she said, shyly, "I can cook pretty well."

It was as if they had re-created a small white corner of the world inside the prisoners' lodge, and yet both knew it could not last.

8

Towards noon, they heard shouting from the west; and a short time after the Indian dogs began their barking and went rushing out of the town.

Caty kept covert watch of her companion. At first he tried to keep on talking — then the restlessness took hold of him. He rose quickly and went to the door. He stayed there quite still, leaning one hand against the jamb. When he spoke his voice had become taut and high.

"There's half a hundred of them coming in."

"Men?"

"Women and children too, and more dogs. It looks like a whole town was coming visiting."

She heard laughter and greetings going back and forth between the parties. Presently they were passing the door of the cabin towards the council house.

"Oh God," said Shoe. "Do you think they're getting up a party for me?"

"Party?" Her echoing him sounded stupid even to herself.

"To burn me."

"No." Her voice was steady, but she did not feel assured.

"I bet they've sent for them so they can see me. Wouldn't you think they'd feel ashamed of making such a fuss over just one prisoner?"

"There's two of us," said Caty, in her steady voice.

"You don't count. A girl. Oh, for God's sake," he cried,

"don't you understand they won't make you run it?"

"Yes, I understand, Henry. But you mustn't think that way. I don't want to see you act scared. I don't want you to let the Indians think a man as big and strong as you is scared of anything they can do. I don't think so."

Their eyes met in the shadowed cabin and Caty felt brave in her heart.

He came over to where she was and sat beside her. His hand reached clumsily for hers and held to it. The din of greetings subsided, and then a new excitement spread over the town, and a little after they saw the Indians streaming out towards the open grassland by the stream.

His voice had tightened once more, but his eyes stayed with hers. "I guess they're making up for another gantlet," he said. "When they take me out, you better stay inside."

Her own voice trembled now.

"Do you want me to?"

"I don't know."

"I'll do whichever you want. I'll stay here inside. Or I'll stand out there where you can see me." She hesitated. "Maybe if you could look at me it would be easier than just seeing them."

"It won't be fun to watch," he said. "Maybe I can't do it. It ain't as if it was the first time."

She squeezed his hand, but did not speak. Then a shadow came through the door and they saw two Indians standing there.

One of them, pointing to Shoe, said, "Come now."

He got up slowly. He did not look back at Caty as he walked out with them.

9

She would not have supposed there were so many Indians. They were drawn up in two long lines, extending nearly two hundred yards from the stream to the beginning of the town. They did not stand close-packed as she had imagined they would, but wide enough apart to have free play for their clubs.

They all had clubs or sticks or tomahawks or knives, as Henry had said. Even a little boy, just old enough to walk, carried a piece of fern to flog the prisoner with. She saw him clear, near the town's limit, his little belly sticking out tight as a drumhead, all of him naked, yelling in his shrill piping beside a fat old squaw.

She saw it all clearly, though the start of the line seemed far away; the braves had taken places in the line strategically, to prevent the prisoner's finding easy stretches. Their laughter had given way. And the sudden hush that came over them as they craned to see him start was violent in its intensity.

It looked so long away, even to her, who could not see their faces. The silence, the still summer heat, the motionless grass and cloudless sky, and the cool brown water of the stream. Only the little child continued his shrill squealing.

Then she saw Henry Shoe at the far end. They had stripped him. His skin was glistening and white for their brown hands. She felt as though a chill from his white skin had reached the whole way between them to touch her heart, and her eyes closed involuntarily.

She wondered what a man could think of there; and then she remembered her pride and opened her eyes wide. She saw him lift his arm, even at that distance seeing the shadow in his armpit. She lifted her own hand as high as she could. Maybe he couldn't see it, she thought, and tore a piece from her shortgown and waved it.

But he had already started running. She knew it before she looked again by the uplifted bedlam of their shouts, the men's whooping and the strident screeches of the squaws. She could no longer catch more than glimpses of him, but each succeeding blow marked plainly where he was. The sticks quivered, poised, and struck. As he passed, the lines crowded together at his back.

She saw him now, running with a blind fury, bull-like, his thick white legs churning and his bare toes digging into the grass. He had blood on his back. He stumbled over a stick but caught himself and hit out with his fist. The squaw screeched and fell backward out of the line, and those beside her laughed.

He was not a real runner, having the short stride that comes from field work, but he was strong as he had told her, and the men now running along the outside of the lines to see him finish did not overtake him. He burst out of the line and came towards the war post by the council house with only the yelping dogs to hinder him and stood there, holding it, his thick chest heaving.

Then he looked for her, finding her still in the cabin door, holding the torn piece from her shortgown. He grinned.

"God, you look funny," he said. "What did you do with your dress?"

The Indians cut him off and the two who had taken him out to the gantlet had to push a way for him through the milling crowd. They were laughing now, and reaching out to pat him with their hands. When they had let him inside the cabin they handed in his clothes. A little later they brought a kettle of stew and the brave who had captured him came in and asked him: —

"You like to go to Niagara?"

"Sure," said Henry. Then he looked at Caty. "How about her?"

"She go too. Fetch eight dollars." The Indian was solemn with satisfaction. "Maybe you fetch ten."

Shoe laughed.

"It's because I'm a man," he said. "We'll be prisoners, but I've heard sometimes they'll let you hire out to work." He helped himself to another chunk of meat. "They ought to be glad in a place like that to get a hired girl like you, though."

Caty looked down at her hands. She did not feel hungry. She had hardly eaten anything. But he was too exuberant to be aware of it.

"Maybe we could get a place together, somewhere in Canada, until the war's over," he said. "Then we'll go back home."

She glanced timidly along his shoulder, and he turned quickly and met her eyes.

"Would that be all right with you?"

"Yes," she said.

He had already turned back to his food. But he stopped

suddenly with it in his fingers. "I couldn't get along without you any more, you know."

Caty was quiet. She was satisfied to let him talk. He no longer depended on her as he had for that short time before; she felt in her heart that he might never again; but she took comfort in the thought of other ways she knew of being useful.

DELIA BORST

THE members of the Seneca war party that had raided Dygartsbush belonged for the most part to the small towns on the upper Genesee River. They were three weeks making the return journey. Only women were left now in the string of burdened captives, and there were fewer of them than had started the long march from their blazing cabins. Old Mrs. Staats had been killed at the night camp from which Honus had made his escape; Caty Breen had been taken off to the north from the headwaters of the Chemung; the two children, Ellen Mitchel and Peter Kelly, had left with the young brave to whom they belonged; and Mrs. Hawyer, who was expecting her first child, had been removed from the string by three of the braves shortly before they came to the wide valley. The remaining women were too wearied from their long, heavy journey even to think about what would happen to them.

Their thoughts were absorbed entirely in themselves; their bruised feet, their torn clothes, the galls on their backs from carrying their unaccustomed burdens, the lack of wholesome food, and their menfolk dead and scalped in the clearings of Dygartsbush.

They dragged along behind the easy walk of the Indians; their voices, murmuring to themselves more than to their companions, were all on one complaining key. They seemed unaware of the clear sky and the south wind drawing down the steep valley. They did not even see the river, a deep blue sinuous cord half hidden by its banks of high natural grass. Only one among them had spirit to lift her eyes and see how beautiful it was.

Delia Borst saw it all before her, as far as her eyes could reach. The grass seemed a green river in itself, with long shallow waves that were running north before the wind; and the trail they were following down and into and through it was like a ford — or, she thought, like the crossing of the Red Sea in the Bible, dividing the high waters of grass. Only, unlike the Israelites, she was entering her bondage, not escaping from it. Her eyes turned to the heads of the Indians in front of her, seeking out the old brave who had captured her at her cabin. She knew that he had spoken of making her his squaw. Young Pete Kelly, who had learned to understand the Indian talk, had told her that three days ago. She lifted her eyes to the sky, unbroken blue, except for a snow-white gull carving his solitary flight into the wind.

She had brief thoughts of her husband. She clung to the thought that he had been away from the settlement the day of the raid; he had not returned to their clearing; and she believed that he must have escaped it entirely. . . . Then they had been married less than a month; now, far into Indian country, she kept telling herself that she was a wife of nearly two months' standing. . . . Sometimes, in quiet moments in the woods, she seemed to hear the sound of his axe; or, at the end of a day's march, she thought of the comfort of his return through the dusk to their cabin. . . . But their cabin was burned, and what little was left of their things she carried on her back; and the pack belonged to the old Indian, as she did herself. . . .

At the head of the line, the old Indian raised his arm to point over the valley. He stood solidly, his stomach jutting out his greasy shirt against the wind, his seamed face impassive as old wood beneath her husband's hat. She followed the direction of his extended finger and saw then, in a bend of the river, beyond a fringe of willow, a trembling haze of smoke against the sky, and through the leaves the bark roofs of Indian cabins.

Her head raised with a little jerk of her round chin. She was a tall girl, as tall as the old Indian, with strong square shoulders and a thick brown rope of hair. Of all the women she alone stood with a straight back under her load.

This was the town, she thought, this small place which they had been heading for through all the endless miles of wilderness. An imperceptible shivering passed over her. She did not close her eyes; she tried to keep her heart thankful that her husband had not been taken with her; but her wide mouth quivered when she thought of him.

The Indians were suddenly full of talk, all pointing to the town, their voices solemn with sententious information. She could not understand what they said to each other though she heard again and again the name "Onondarha." Then she saw that the old Indian was watching her with his small dark eyes. She forced her own not to waver. He pressed his lips together, forcing the lower outward, and swung away abruptly down the steep slope, and for those last few moments, while she followed with the other captives, she said over and over to herself, "My name is Mrs. John Borst. My name is Mrs. John Borst."

2

Times came later when the memory of that clear day of her entering into the Indian town brought a deeper aching to her heart than the thought of her burned cabin. It was the last moment in which she could remember the girl who had been Delia Borst. Now she could not imagine herself as the same person. Not even one day when she slipped away from the cornfield belonging to the women of her lodge and went to the edge of the river. She stared for a long time at the face riding the glassy slide of water close to the bank. She could see the same slight arching of the brows that had been hers, the same roundness of the chin, brown of the eyes, and curved meeting of the lips.

It was the kind of face John Borst had said a man could not keep himself away from. The recollection of the words, and the unexpectedness with which he had said them in the first days of their meeting, overwhelmed her. For an instant she saw the face that watched her from the water, the still eyes, the weatherburn on the cheeks; then she could no longer see it. She was crouching down in the shelter of the tall grass, holding her head tight, as if by main strength she could keep her sanity.

How long she crouched there under her bitter stream of thoughts she never knew. But step by step her mind retraced the occurrences of those first days.

The night of their arrival, sitting with Martha Dygart, Mrs. Empie, and the other women in a small unlighted cabin used for prisoners, she listened to the singing and powwow from the council house. The beating of the drum underneath all other sound was like a pulse become articulate. They got used to it after a while, and they talked in unconnected sequences about what the Indians would do with them. Mrs. Empie seemed to be the only one who had done any thinking about Indians. "I calculate this town is a little one way off from the main towns. We been heading south of west. I calculate not many British troops come this way."

One asked, "What difference does it make?"

"I guess it means they won't send us to Niagara, because I calculate that's quite a ways off from here. Probably they'll keep us to do work for them."

"Do they ever . . ." The woman's voice shook and dropped. She began again, "Do they ever — kill women prisoners?"

Mrs. Empie's dry, hard, common-sense voice, that sounded just as she looked, toil-bent, with all the natural sap worked out of her, was easy to believe. Nobody thought to question where she got her knowledge. "If you get sick so you ain't worth nothing to them, maybe, they'll kill you. Now and then I've heard tell of them making a woman run the gantlet. But it ain't usual."

Delia found herself also questioning.

"Do they ever marry white women?"

"Who's that talking?" Mrs. Empie asked.

"Me, Delia Borst."

"You're the good-looker, ain't you?" Mrs. Empie sounded as though she knew where good looks in a woman went to and had watched them go. "I don't know, it ain't usual." She blew her breath out in the dark. "They ain't like white men — my husband told me that. He said, 'Mellicent,' he said, 'if you ever get caught by the Indians you don't need to be scared that way!' 'No,' I said to him, 'nor of any other man either now, the way I've had to work for you!' But he said no, that Indians didn't hardly never molest a woman, that way. So you needn't get skeery."

"I'm not," said Delia.

"No, I reckon you don't want to be. Me, I'm scared this moment."

"Pete Kelly told me the old Indian talked about marrying me," said Delia.

"I don't know nothing about that."

"I'd die first, before I done that." The voice was hushed and passionate, and full of terror.

"Would you?" said Mrs. Empie. "How'd you stop it, I'd like to know."

"I don't know." The voice broke, then lifted sharply. "But I would."

Delia wished she knew which woman it was speaking.

"Well," said Mrs. Empie, "I don't calculate there's nothing left any more for me to get back for. But if there was, I'd see to it I managed to get back if it took me half my life; and I'd keep my mouth shut how I did it, too."

She added after a minute, "That's what we'd better do, too. Keep our mouths shut. When an Indian gets mad, he gets so awful sullen and I guess he don't know himself how far he's going with it."

*   *   *

Delia remembered it now, the dry sane voice and the darkness and the dry, light thudding of the drum. She had not seen Mrs. Empie again for a long time for Mrs. Empie, like the other women, had been taken to one of the other towns. (There were six towns scattered in the small steep tributary valleys of that section of the Genesee.) Then Delia met her once more at the New Year's feast, when Gasotena strangled the white dog. The woman had not changed; she came in carrying a load for her masters; her body bent, but moving with the same dry strength. She seemed to have no inclination for visiting, even to the extent that the slaves were allowed to mingle, and by then Delia had become shy of meeting other white women. . . .

Lying in the grass beside the river, Delia remembered how she had been adopted. She did not know what it was that was happening. Gasotena made a speech in front of her, and then the head woman of the house stepped out from the crowd and smiled and patted Delia's arm and led her away.

The other women of the Indian household joined them inside, chattering as they examined her tattered clothes; and then picked out many of their own best things to dress her in. It was hard to find anything wide enough to cover her shoulders, so they had to leave her shortgown on her, but they gave her one of her own white blankets and with the blue Indian skirt and quilled moccasins she looked like a tall, straight-standing Indian girl. Her warm heart swelled and tears came to her eyes. They seemed so friendly to her and so kind. She said thank you to them one by one, until the youngest, understanding her, said, "*Hi-ne-a-weh,*" whereupon they all beamed, pointing to her lips, until she said stumblingly, "*Hi-ne-a-weh.*"

She had no idea of how talkative and kindly the Indian women would seem. When the head woman came over to take her hand and lead her to one of the fires burning on the earthen floor, her anxiousness to please them made her almost tremulous. She quickly comprehended what they wanted of her, mixing the cornmeal and water under their direction and baking the unleavened nocake on a flat, heated stone. As soon as it was done, with a smiling face, the head woman signified that Delia was to carry it to an old woman who, in spite of the heat, sat huddled in furs and blankets, unspeaking, with only her bright eyes alive. The old woman accepted the cake with her twiglike fingers. She stirred, faintly, but her voice was low and rather hoarse, like a croaking bird's. "*Go-ah-wuk.*" Delia knew now it meant "daughter"; then she did not know, but stood smilingly before the old woman thinking how very old her memory must be. She had the look of the ancient, with young eyes as though they looked on youthful landscapes and young faces long since forgotten by people with better memories. Even when the head woman took Delia's arm and led her to the central south side cubicle and spread a deerskin for her on the low platform, she did not realize that she had just been married.

When night came, and she discovered what had happened to her, there was no turning back. In the double row of cubicles running down each side of the log house, with the acrid smoke-smell lading the dark air and the fires buried, people were lying all around her. There were eight families — men and squaws and children — and the ancient woman who seemed not to sleep, but sat upright, breathing her light breaths, her eyes reflecting the one faint spot of red.

During the dark succeeding hours she lay unstirring except for the heavy slow beating of her heart. She could not think; she could not remember; she was only conscious of the breathing Indians round her and the restive sound of dog paws in the dry weeds outside the walls, of the night sky and the limitless woods beneath which she had traveled step by step to that one helpless moment of her life.

3

Delia was brought to herself by the sound of stealthy approach through the high grass. One of the dogs from her own house had sniffed out her trail. He dropped his haunches and lolled his tongue at her between the green blades. He was motionless, then, except for the pink tongue; and his slanted foxy eyes examined her with the critical detachment of a wild thing.

Delia lifted herself slowly to her feet. The grass tips swayed dizzily against the blue sky. She had an irrational, quick, unhappy thought of John Borst's amazement if he could ever see such grass. It reached above her head, even when she stood straight, and there were places where the Indians said it grew over ten feet tall. She pushed her way through it along the little footpath, hearing the dry pat of the dog's feet behind her own.

As she emerged from the grass she could see the squaws still weeding the long rows of hilled young corn and squash. But she had no heart left for longer working under the hot sun. Her fit of weeping had exhausted her; she felt as though all the strength she ever had had been washed out of her; and she could not bear the thought that any of the Indian women could see how she had given way. She still had pride enough never to let them see her own humiliation. But she thought of the house, now, as a refuge. At this hour of the afternoon it would be empty. All the women were in the field, the men out hunting or fishing, and the children off on their endless games of war party played with blunt-headed arrows and lances. Their voices, made shrill in the clearness of the day, whooped on the higher slopes. Not even a papoose would be left, for they were in their baby frames, hanging from branches near where their mothers worked.

The winter months and the succeeding spring had made the house familiar, comforting with its feeling of four solid barriers against the wilderness. The hewn-log, windowless walls were low, meeting the narrow eaves of the curving roof. It looked no different from the other houses irregularly scattered among the trees; but to her it had become her place of home. She pushed open the swinging door that scraped a track for itself on the dirt floor, stepped in, and closed it.

For an instant, she stood looking down the narrow length, where the four bars of sunlight entering the smoke vents were made misty by the last remnants of the morning fires. The spread deerskins in the cubicles; the bearskin robes; the bark barrels in their appointed corners; the cooking dishes hanging from the uprights; the last few braids of corn ears, left after winter, depending from the rafters; all the clutter of domestic welfare contributed to her sense of refuge — they were things to know and use. Even her own cubicle which Gasotena shared was made intimate for her by her workbasket and needlecase, her own few clothes and the unfinished moccasins she was learning to fashion with such ineptitude and labor. His belongings seemed less personal — his trade axe, two spears, and the queer pagan war club that he used for ceremonials; the container holding his silver brooches, bands, and beaded clothes.

She sat down wearily on the edge, feeling herself at rest. "Daughter." The voice was low and slightly hoarse. Delia quickly lifted her eyes. She had forgotten the ancient woman who never stirred from the house. For an instant her cheeks brightened with resentment; but as she looked at the lined, dry, dark skin stretched upon the bone, she met the woman's eyes, large and dark and quick with sympathy, as though a lost spring of humanity had welled up through long-forgotten channels.

"*Ucsote.*" Delia gave her the title of Grandmother, and felt her own heart quicken in response. She rose dutifully to wait on her, for the old woman had become almost entirely helpless through the winter.

The old woman watched her with upturned eyes, and after a moment, in which she seemed to have been collecting her energies for a new word, she said, "Sit down by me."

Delia obeyed, sitting close. The old woman's breathing was so insubstantial that, though Delia's shoulder touched the cone of blankets, she could detect no stirring. Not even when the old woman turned her head. Before speaking, she faced forward again, as if the effort of looking to one side was a drain upon her strength.

"Why do you grieve?" she asked.

It was the first personal remark Delia had ever heard the old woman make. She was too surprised to answer, or for a moment to think of its application to herself. But the old woman, after more quiet breathing, parted her thin seamed lips and said, "You are young and warm. You should not grieve."

"I am not grieving," Delia said. Though she could see only the profile, it suddenly occurred to her that the old woman's features did not have the tribal resemblance found in the other inhabitants of the town. Through her ancient prescience the old woman seemed to understand.

"A woman cannot help the things of God." For God, she used the name Ataentsic, and Delia, though she spoke still haltingly, knew enough of the language to be surprised; for Ataentsic, the oldest god, was a woman, the Moon; and in the village all other Indians addressed Areskoui, the Sun.

"No, Ucsote," Delia said. "But you must not tire yourself with talking to me."

The old woman, however, seemed to gain strength as she talked. Her dry lips closed inward, making her chin jut out. "I am tired of being still, Goahwuk." She stopped. "I wish to know why you grieve. It is because you have married my son." She stirred and for a moment a shadow of irritation crossed her sunken face. "My grandson," she corrected herself, explaining, "It is so long since he was born."

Delia forgot the old woman's decrepitude. She bowed her head, looking at her hands. The sun from the smoke vent fell upon them in her lap and touched her dark brown hair. The quality of the old woman's voice did not change; but her lips became fuller, and her eyes were gentle.

"I was brought to this town when I was young. I belonged to the Cherokee nation, daughter. It was more than a lifetime ago, for I am very old."

She paused for a long time, regained breath and strength. Then haltingly, she went on to talk, telling in snatches how she had been captured in an early Iroquois raid and brought to Onondarha. Since her coming the town had changed sites four times. Then the houses were all of bark. They changed whenever the infestation of insects became unbearable. Now with hewn-log walls it was easier to make a house last longer. Also it kept out some of the wind in winter, which was good for bones that barely clung together at the joints. She had been adopted in the Joasseh clan, the Herons.

Delia was barely able to follow the dry patter of her words. But she seemed to see the fourteen-year-old girl brought into the town. "I was married to a chief," the old woman said. "They took him to another town. Then Gasotena, the chief of this place, wished to have a squaw.

He would take me, but I said I was married. They then sent to the other town and my husband was burned. So I married Gasotena, the chief man of this town. I grieved like you."

The silence was broken by the distant shrilling of the children at play.

"My son was born after my fifteenth spring. I knew he would come when the blackberries began to ripen. I named him Little Otter. When his father died he took his name, High-Grass, Gasotena. He was a good man. I have not been sorry. I can sit here now and see my children. I watch them sometimes. I wonder if they remember I am Cherokee. I do not speak of it. I did not think of it until you married my grandson. He has become a good chief."

During her long pause she seemed to struggle with herself, and mechanically Delia leaned forward to help her shift the blankets. The hand came forth slowly and took Delia's in the stiff twiglike fingers. Slowly the old woman turned it over, looking at the whiter palm, and Delia looked at it with her.

"It is a warm hand," the old woman said.

Delia choked a sob.

"It is white, Ucsote. And I was married, too."

"You should have said so, daughter."

"I did not know."

"Perhaps it was better. This town is far from white people's places of settling. If Gasotena knew he would have to journey back and kill your husband to make it right. Perhaps it is better for some things to be wrong. Perhaps you will not be like me but go back some time."

"Ucsote, I cannot now."

The eyes suddenly grew moist.

"Are you like me also in that?"

Delia nodded.

"The white women are different in what they want. But they cannot escape what happens to them either. That is the same with all women wherever they are born."

Delia drew a long, shuddering breath, and the twig-like fingers tightened on her hand with a shadow of strength.

"I could not go back," she said, "but after a while I did not want to."

"I can't go back — now," Delia said.

"Why not, daughter?"

"Could you have left your son?"

"Why are you ashamed? Because you are white?" There was a faint reproof in the ancient voice. "If you stayed when the time came to go, you would still be white. It is better for him to be an Indian, perhaps. I have thought about it since you came. My grandson wished to marry you, and I could see you were a good woman. I did not say no. You have been good to me. Now, I have finished speaking."

The hand slowly withdrew and Delia closed the blankets over the old woman.

Far away the dogs began barking. The old woman spoke for the last time, with quiet pride. "All the men of this house are good hunters. My grandson has killed a deer."

4

Gasotena, puffing, brought in a young dry doe, carrying the carcass whole, with an air of pride. To others of the men who had begun to straggle home, he explained how he had started and let her go, because he saw she was heading towards the town. Then he tracked her and shot her about a mile from home. He hadn't had luck like that for three years, he said, dumping the carcass down near the skin beam and setting about the skinning of it. Hunting wasn't what it used to be when he was a boy.

The young men listened to his speech austerely, but the older ones nodded, saying it took the old hands to find the easy does. They did not laugh, but looked sidelong at one another, ignoring the young men and making stomach chuckles.

Standing in the door, Delia watched their brown sweaty backs gathered together on the ground. She would have to work the skin on the round beam tomorrow, she would have to rub it with the brains tonight. Her stomach turned inexplicably, for she had not minded working deer hides heretofore. It was the nearest thing to spinning that Indian women had to do; once she had learned the trick of taking off the grain, her mind was released from the work of her hands.

Now she watched Gasotena's knife skillfully laying back the hide. As he bared the legs, he cut loose the needle bone with two short cuts, so swiftly it was like a miracle to see the needle in his hand. He announced that he had met a Toryohne man back of the west falls on the beech ridge. The man had told him the Wolf house of his village, Owaiski, were planning a war party within a week and would wait near the forks for half a day if any of the Onondarha young men wished to join them.

There was a long silence after he had spoken, all looking towards him to see whether he had made up his own mind. But of that he kept silence, finished the skinning and cutting up of the carcass, and handed out the sections to members of his own house while the women of the other houses looked on enviously — wishing that their own men were as good providers.

He dropped the two small needle bones on her workbox for her to dry and fashion and eye; then he sat down on the edge of the cubicle. When she set the pot down before him and handed him his ladle, he thanked her gravely. He had drawn his blanket over his naked back, but he still wore the hat.

Delia seldom thought of its origin any more for it had long since lost its identity with John Borst. The brim sagged from a winter of snow and there were two slits in the crown through which the quill of a feather could be passed when Gasotena felt ceremonious. The very smell of it was Indian. But it was the best hat that had ever come into the town, and Gasotena would boast endlessly about its prowess in holding the rain off the top of his head; it had acquired a character in his imagination; he talked about it as if it were himself. He never took it off unless to lie down when he was sober.

That evening he kept it on after his meal, and as Delia set about making a cake of the deer's brains and moss to work the hide with, she could see him walking underneath the hat towards the council house. One of his nieces, who had married an ambitious brave from Owaiski, came out of the house to help her. She said, "Now there will be a council."

Delia nodded. "It is kind of you to help me, cousin."

The girl moved her eyes demurely sidewise.

"Ucsote talked to your husband now," she observed. "He has gone forth very pleased."

Delia flushed. "I do not need help."

"Ucsote spoke to me also." The girl's name was Deowuhyeh. She was young and soft-spoken and quick to smile. She did not meet Delia's eyes. "My cousin is not like us," she said, softly. "Ucsote said so."

The task she was doing blurred under Delia's eyes. She felt the same rush of warmth in her heart that she had felt earlier in the house. For the first time since she had been taken captive she realized that she had a friend. It seemed like a miracle that one so old, of another race, could understand such little things. She glanced hastily at the girl beside her. Deowuhyeh (Among the Reeds) was bending with her at their work, but her lips curved as she smiled. And for a little while the two young women worked together without speaking.

Soon, however, Deowuhyeh's eyes turned towards the council house from which a single voice issued in a long, rhythmic exposition. As the twilight made encroachments in the town, they could see the glow of the fire through the door and the squatting men or their shadows that leaned backward on the walls.

"It is a war council," the girl whispered. "There are no women." As Delia said nothing, she asked, "Do you not hope they go?"

"No," said Delia.

"Gasotena will want to go now," said the girl. "He talked with my husband in our house. I wish my husband to go. We need money now. The man from Owaiski said the British paid eight dollars for a scalp as they did last year. Gasotena is pleased. He said he would need a better musket now to teach his son to shoot." She smiled once more, then sobered, creasing her forehead prettily, to quote her husband, Ganowauges. "My husband has said it is a good time for the men to go. Hunting is poor this month, but there is food enough for the women with the berries ripening. He is wise, though young. It is a good year for berries. Many men will go if Gasotena does. He knows the trails to the white settlements. He is a great man."

5

During the ensuing days, though nothing happened, Delia became conscious of a growing excitement in the town. Hardly anyone went into the woods. They hung around the houses all day long: the older men holding conferences in the sunshine, talking slowly, one by one; the younger men looking on with hot, impatient eyes until they could stand it no longer and went to the river where they practised throwing their tomahawks at a stake.

The women acted as though they did not know what was going on, until they found themselves alone at their work in the cornfields. Then they would begin an excited, chattering speculation about the number of men the war party would make up to, where they would head for, and what luck there would be. Those wives who were positive of their men's joining mentioned them proudly and so they formed an accurate notion of the number that would leave their own town. Some went visiting to other towns to see relatives in their own clans, and these brought back vague statistics. They figured out that it would be a small party that would join the Owaiski men, the largest number coming from Onondarha. But of other details they could only make a guess.

A few of the older women mentioned names they had heard. Honoagoneh, Schenectady; Dayaogeh, Fort Herkimer — but with no notion of where they were or what they stood for. Their main concern was with the wealth that might be brought back in salable scalps or plunder.

As Delia listened to their voiced opinions, or returned to the house to cook Gasotena's food and felt the intensified excitement in the town, her thoughts moved irrationally. She would awaken in the middle of the night and lie still, listening to Gasotena's heavy breath on the far wall of the cubicle and experiencing an almost hysterical conviction that he would be killed and she herself consequently released. She would start trembling. Once she prayed that it might happen; but then she felt ashamed by an aware-

ness of the ancient woman's sleepless eyes as she kept
her endless erect vigil across the passage. Again, she passed
long waking hours entirely concerned in a kind of dreamy
awareness of the growing life she carried, as though in a
still way she were becoming for the first time acquainted
with her own body. At other times, waking or sleeping, a
vision of her own burnt cabin back in Dygartsbush would
rise before her, with John Borst standing by himself and
Gasotena stalking him, like a stealthy brown fat bear,
through the high weeds.

But the news that broke unexpectedly over the whole
Genesee Valley reached Onondarha on the fourth of July.
That very morning it was discovered that the war post
before the council house had been painted with new red,
and the whole town was expectant of Gasotena's war
whoop which would begin the war dance, for he had
disappeared and surreptitious examination of his cubicle
showed them that his ceremonial finery had gone.

The runners came in the third hour before noon. A
yelping dog down the valley gave them the alarm. For an
instant only the dogs heeded them — they raised slowly
from the ground, ears pointed and noses at work. Then in
one body they streamed out of the town, leaving a low float-
ing of dust in their wake. At the same moment a couple of
boys fishing in a bend of the river lifted their shrill yelling
and all the town could see the runners.

At first two specks in the high grass, shaven heads and
braided locks unfeathered, then two pairs of shoulders,
glistening with sweat, and at last they could see them
plainly following the river trail, holding themselves to-

gether, keeping their even pace — a trot that seemed slow
when one first saw it but that brought the runners forward towards the house with surprising swiftness.

Both men were naked except for breechclouts, belts, and
moccasins. They came into the town moving strongly,
only their deep breathing showing the length they had
come. Their faces streamed and the sweat on their oiled
coppery hides stood up in drops.

They went straight to the council house, not speaking;
and the door opened for them, and the people saw Gasotena in his full regalia, facing the open door, his red war
hatchet in his right fist and the antique musket in his left.
His flowered calico shirt was thick with brooches, the full
sleeves fastened at the wrists with brooches, and a scarlet
beaded sash hung down his blue trouser legs. He had
fastened the eagle feather and fox-down puff to the
crown of his hat, but under it he wore the silver head-
band, so that the hat perched loosely and unsteadily on
his head. In the shadow of the brim, the yellow and vermilion striping of his face was featureless.

The older men, followed by the young, crowded in
behind the runners and the women pushed towards the
open door. Delia was left alone in the open space with the
yapping dogs about her. Only silence came from the council house; it lasted till the dogs had stilled, and then the
only sound for a long time was the whine of a locust
from a great maple tree on the edge of the woods.

As she stood alone, with her eyes moving restlessly from
the council house to the other houses, from the backs of
the close-crowded women to the solemn stares of the

younger children watching from the grass and bushes, a
queer feeling of disaster assailed Delia. She heard one of
the runners beginning his message. He spoke in a ringing voice, slowly and rhythmically. And suddenly what he
was saying became understandable to Delia. They brought
a message from the British Colonel Butler at Canadasaga.
The rebels had collected a great army far down the Susquehanna. They had another army in the Mohawk. These
the Colonel, Butler, had been watching with spies. Now
there was no doubt where these two armies were coming.
The army on the Susquehanna was already above Wyo-
ming. There could be no doubt that the rebels were coming
to destroy the Indian country. Colonel Butler's army was
ready to move down against them when the time came —
he now sent runners to all the Seneca towns to call for men
to fight.

The stillness now was broken by a long-drawn, high-
pitched murmur from the Indian women. Then Gasotena's
voice after an interval asked how many men the rebels
had. The runner said it was not sure, but there were many
men in the army, twice as many as all the men of fighting
age in the whole Long House. They were also bringing
cannon. And again the high murmur of sound came out
of the women with a deeper note, this time from the men.

In the ensuing quiet, Delia became aware of the hard
beating of her heart. She felt the blood rising to her face;
it filled her body even to her fingers' ends. A profound
conviction of the army's coming even to Onondarha for an
instant overwhelmed her and she forgot everything in
the belief that she would soon be home.

All her senses became sharp and quick. She saw the two runners come out of the council house, catch stride together, and head south up the valley. She saw dismay and fear and wonder on the faces of the women. It seemed to her that she could hear the individual strokes of separate wings to make the endlessly repeated sound of the hot-weather bird. One of the women must have been drying deer meat in the sun, for Delia could smell it. And then she heard Gasotena's voice uplifted in the council house. She could imagine him in his outlandish clothes, with his horrible face and his outthrusting stomach, standing in the circle of old men; but her mind was captured by the vision of the army coming through the wilderness.

She listened to his words without excitement, mechanically translating them in her mind.

He spoke very briefly of the founding of the Long House, the League of the Six Nations, repeating the roll call of the founders; the names, sonorous, came slowly from his lips. He told how the Seneca nation were made the keepers of the western door of the Long House and how it had never been invaded through their precinct. The Mohawks had been surrounded by the rebel people and forced to leave their country. The Oneidas had gone with the rebels, and the Tuscaroras had never been fighting men. Now through their country, from the inside of the Long House itself, from the one direction which they had never feared, the enemy were coming to destroy their country. There had been talk of a war party to take scalps; now he would talk of a war he would go on. . . . The corn was high in the fields, soon it would tassel. The beans had bloom on the vines and the squash leaves were spread wide like the wings of flying birds. This was their food for the winter. These were the fields they had planted. He saw the apple trees and the peach trees. They were old as the town was. Where the town had been, there were apple trees that still bore fruit, marking the site of the town. This was the land their ancestors found for them. This was the land on which they built the Long House. This was the land of the men, they who had hunted over it. This was the land of the women, this was the land they planted. This was the land of the children, who were learning the axe and the arrow, who crawled on the floors of the lodges. Areskoui, the Sun, he had fashioned it. He had planted the fish in the rivers; he had put the deer on the hills; he had made the three sisters first grow, the corn and the bean and the squash, so the Indian might live through the winter. He had built the sky over the world so that there might be rain and wind and warmth, and he had loosed the birds in its emptiness. This was the land where they lived. Let them defend it. . . .

When he ceased, one after another the old men spoke, asking that the young men go forth, speaking of the love of war that completed a man's soul, and of the strength of the British who would help them, and of the covenant chain with the British King, that the Senecas had never broken. The army of the rebels came from a far distance; they would be lost in the woods. Their numbers were greater than the pigeons, but pigeons were birds without wisdom and could be killed without arrows.

To Delia, who had for a moment felt queerly moved by Gasotena's words, the speeches were monotonous. She moved out of the house and went into the woods as though to gather a faggot; but really to be solitary. Her one thought was of when the army would come. Would they know of the white women held by the Indians; would they trouble to look for them?

When she had gathered her faggot, she came out on a slope above the town, looking down on the rounded grey bark roofs, and the congregated heads of the Indians. They were before the council house and the red war post and Gasotena was emerging from the doorway. His face lifted; and the war whoop rose out of his painted face in an almost visible syllable. Before it had finished ringing the whole town took it up, setting the dogs howling and barking, and Gasotena began the steps of the War Dance towards the post. His stamping heels kept time with the beating of the drum. He leaned forward, crouching, then reared himself and began his war song. For three minutes his voice was alone over the crowd; then came the war whoop and with full force he buried his tomahawk in the post and called for men to follow him. Without waiting he went into his stamping dance round the post, and a young man whooped and sprang in behind him, while the women shrilly applauded.

Suddenly, to Delia, in the full glare of the noon sun, they looked pathetic with their painted faces and outlandish clothes. What could they do against an army? She shouldered her faggot and made her way slowly back to her own house.

6

The town without the men became still as a forgotten
town. After the first week, the women went about their
tasks without much talk. The few old men remaining
fished and the oldest of the boys hunted for deer. But they
got little meat. The raspberries and then the blackberries
ripened and were picked. The maturing squash were cut
and dried. Once one of the boys discovered the nesting place
of a large flock of pigeons and the town feasted for several
days. But no word came from the east, no runners passed
up the valley until towards the middle of the month a
band of Indians suddenly appeared from the southwest.
There were men, women and children, even dogs, in the
party. They were footsore and hungry. They came from
a town on the Alleghany, which they called the Oheeyo,
and they reported its burning by an army of the rebels.
Looking at the members of them who belonged to the
Heron clan and who therefore lodged themselves in her
house, Delia saw in their dark faces the same dismay and
hopelessness that she remembered on the faces of her
woman neighbors captured in Dygartsbush. They told the
same story — the sudden appearance of the white troops;
the ineffectual stand of the men down the river; the burning of their houses and fields. When they looked out on
the corn tassels in the Onondarha planting, their eyes became dull.

The house was hard put to feed them all; but no one

complained. They were like one family, waiting for news from the south. One of the arriving young men was sent to the east to find the British and the Indians with them; the others scouted in the southwest. Finally, at the end of the month, they brought word that the army had gone back down the river, and the scouts returned and then went east themselves to join the British.

But early in September, some men of the town came back. The tale they brought was terrible. All the town packed into the council house to hear of the battle on the Chemung where the Indians were routed by cannon and an army of men four times as great as the British and Indians combined.

There was no withstanding them at all. The Colonel, Butler, was retreating day by day northwestward to fall back on Niagara, and the great rebel force followed, burning every town, cutting down the corn and trampling the fields with their herd of cattle, even felling the fruit trees.

A moan like the wind passing over a hemlock wood rose from the Indian women. The men were still. The speaker went on: Inhabitants of all the towns were falling back on the Genesee; and word had been sent to Genesee Castle even to abandon the fields and houses.

"Are we to go?" a woman asked.

The speaker shook his head. "Gasotena tells us to wait." The rebels had turned north from Catherinestown; the fall was coming; they might not find the six towns on the Genesee.

7

Delia forced her way out through the door. Not since that day by the river had she felt so shaken. During those two months, she had sustained herself with her belief that the army would surely come. Now as profound a conviction that Gasotena was right made her hopeless.

She entered the deserted house to find, as she had before, the old eyes of the ancient woman watching her. She had learned to feel a genuine affection for the Ucsote, and now she suddenly gave way, crying unashamedly before her. In her hope of rescue, she had not allowed herself to think of Gasotena and the coming winter. She could not help it now. She could wish he might die, but it would do no good. She was as helpless as a leaf on a tree, waiting for the autumn wind.

The old woman looked down on her bowed head, sitting in her motionlessness, only moving her eyes. This storm of weeping made her uneasy. Indian women concealed grief, unless they wept for a departed one.

She whispered finally, "He is not dead."

As Delia lifted her face, she went on, "It is better for you that he is not dead. If he died, you would have no rights in this house any more. Because you were adopted you could live here. That is all. All your things would belong to the house again."

"I do not care about *things*."

"I know it is true. Yet if you went back now your

child would be born in a white place and it would still be part Indian. Are the white people kinder to part-Indian children than we are? Would they give it rights in property? Here it belongs to the house it is born in and yet it is part white. But that will be forgotten. There is Gayantwaka, the Cornplanter; he is half white."

There was no answer for Delia to make. She knew that if the child were born the sight of its face would always make her unhappy. With her uncanny understanding of another's thought, the old woman continued, "Is it a good thing for a child to know his mother is ashamed of bearing him? My daughter, there are things to consider. With the child in you, you are part Indian, in the part that he is. Would your white husband relish the wife that is part Indian?" Her seamed lips grew tender, and her whispering voice was kind. "You have been good to me. You have been good to these poor people who are our kin. You have a good heart. I love you as my daughter. Let your heart be good, daughter. That is the purpose of a woman. You are yet warm and young. There is time." She let her eyes close. But after a while she said, "I have finished. *Hano.*"

Her old head sank. She never spoke to Delia again. When, at the end of the month, Gasotena led home the half-starved, half-mad warriors of the town, she spoke one more sentence: "Now the Long House is broken." That night she died. But she was so swathed in blankets that no one realized she was dead until a dog in the dawn snuffed her in passing and stopped suddenly to howl.

8

With the passage of days the extent of disaster gradually was made apparent. Except for the few small towns on the upper Genesee, and a few west of the river, the American army under General Sullivan had destroyed the Seneca country — not only the towns, but the orchards and fields; not only the growing things, but the caches of dried corn laid down to last two years. And the second expedition under Colonel Brodhead had done the same thing in the south.

At Onondarha and the neighboring villages, the inhabitants saw a good half of their corn crop used up by refugees as soon as it was harvested. And though these people soon passed to the northwest to Niagara, summoned by the head men of the nation, until late into the winter lone families straggled in from time to time, poorly dressed, starving, and ill — families that had been away in the autumn and had bravely attempted to return to their old house sites, and had found even the game swept out of the country by the marching army of eight thousand men.

As her time drew near, it became more and more Delia's concern to look out for the little children of these poor dispossessed folk, with their faces clay-colored from cold and lack of food. She made friends easily, as her heart warmed to them, and they were fascinated by the whiteness of her skin, and the brownness of her hair, and the lowness of her voice.

Sometimes it seemed to Delia the gathering strength of

the child's life-spark in her made her, as the old woman had said, actually part Indian. She began to talk more freely with the women of the house, asking their guidance. She was hardly aware of Gasotena sitting in their cubicle, smoking his dry tobacco, during the long winter days, while the snow pellets fingered the bark roof and the wind drew moaningly across the smoke holes. When he presented her with choice marten skins for the baby she took them to cure as her ordinary due, and he was pleased to let her so accept them.

By the turn of the year the food had got so low that the whole town went on rations. In the houses everyone shared alike according to the Indian usage, but now the houses joined and if a deer was brought in, it had to be equally shared by every living person. The dogs became ghostly in their emaciation, what few survived the stewpots for breeding. It was a bad year for game and the deer moved far into the mountains southward to yard.

But Delia kept well and strong, and one day the old woman who had succeeded to the Ucsote's name and position said to her, "It is as though she had not departed, but had grown young again in your body."

In February, during the bitter freeze which that year made the ice so thick on the river that it was nearly impossible to fish through it, Delia's time came. She arose in the hour before dawn and left the house. The stars were paling in the grey sky and a faint sifting of flakes came down without clouds, as if the wind that blew so strong had carried them from an infinite distance and dropped them, spent, upon the town. The track upward from the door was hard to climb.

The head woman and the girl, Deowuhyeh, hearing her efforts, rose and came after, the one bringing bearskins and the other a great faggot of wood. They fought with her through the snow to the tiny cabin and built a fire on the snow that had sifted in. The smoke for a while balked at the smoke vent, and the heat was a limited globe held close to the flame. Deowuhyeh crouched before it, her cheeks round with blowing, blinking her eyes against the smoke. The head woman took Delia's arm and kept her walking round and round the fire. She had no mercy on her, and even though Delia begged would not let her rest.

But the fire finally roared high. The heat expanded almost to the walls. The snow on the floor melted back from the burning sticks and the smoke began to seep through the vent. None of the three women spoke, there was no sound but the rapid crackle of the burning sticks. Deowuhyeh held the robes up before the flames to take the chill from them and then made a place on the platform where Delia might rest when her child was born. . . .

It was snowing heavily then, but the flakes were big and soft and fell without a wind. Delia lay on the bear robes, covered to her eyes against the cold, her eyes following the smoke's seepage through the vent while she wondered how far it might rise.

The baby that she had wrapped clumsily on his board under the head woman's tuition lay buried under the blankets with her, a shapeless hard small lump.

"He is a fine strong boy, though small," said the head woman.

Deowuhyeh smiled.

"Already he has made his war whoop."

In spite of her exhaustion Delia smiled back when she thought of that thin high single crying whine. To call it the war whoop was comical and like Deowuhyeh, who liked to laugh. When the head woman said, "You should think of his baby name while you rest," Delia was not conscious of what the head woman said for a minute. For it seemed to her that there was a wildness in the baby's cry after all, like something she had heard at dusk before a snowfall. She had heard it far up one of the valleys and it had frightened her even in the house crowded with Indians. Seeing her troubled face, Gasotena had explained that it was a panther — *Haace,* he called it. She repeated the word more to herself than the others. But both the women clapped their hands.

"Ha-ace, panther. The little panther. It is a good name."

The head woman's eyes grew brooding and prophetic.

"It is a good name for a fighting man. He will go out some day and though his name will be changed in manhood, there will be people who remember that his mother called him Ha-ace."

Her voice lifted abruptly to the high Indian octave, and her whole face was bitterly transformed.

"He will remember the time he was born, and he will be a great warrior against the white people." She glanced at Deowuhyeh and found her face afire with the vision too. "Like another Gayantwaka," she said.

Then they looked at Delia; but she lay still with her head turned to the hood of the baby frame. Her eyes were closed. But her full lips curved, softening the new lines in her face.

MARTHA DYGART

It was a year and three months since Martha Dygart had been captured, but she did not think of that. She did not even think of where the Indians were going, or why they had all moved out of Chenandoanes. She had never been a quick-witted woman. Even after a year among the Indians she had not learned to understand their language. A few words she knew, like *wood, water, dirty, fire, corn, hoe, work,* and *beat.* They were the words that counted most in a slave's life in an Indian town. Gekeahsawsa, the Wildcat, the head woman of the lodge, would point to the task in hand and speak a word, like a man ordering a dog, and if there were any hesitation or stupidity, she would set on with the ever-ready hickory club. And if the slave showed her teeth as a dog might, there were all the women of the household ready to rush screeching to Gekeahsawsa's aid.

Now she could hear the strong steady tread of the woman behind her and could imagine her blocky legs, her thick chest more like a man's than a woman's, and the opaque black eyes with smoke-sore scars about the lids. She always kept just behind, driving her slave as one might drive a pack mare; and though the load she herself carried was nearly as heavy, she still managed to handle her hickory gad whenever there was a sign of loitering.

At such moments of explosive rage, the veins swelled on her temples, her heavy cheeks seemed to fill, and the sweetish Indian smell of her body strengthened offensively as the body scent of certain animals is said to act. The slave had long ago learned to take warning from that increased intensity of odor.

She looked gaunt and ill-fed under her unwieldy pack. She walked slowly, planting each foot with care in the hard-worn slot of the Indian trail. Her hands grasping the brow strap beside her face to steady the load showed her bare arms through the torn sleeves of her overdress. It was no more than a rag hardly covering her burned skin. Her brown hair, braided like an Indian's, was matted and dull.

For miles she did not lift her lustreless eyes from the trail. She might have been taken for an Indian herself if she had looked a little less ragged, dirty, and ill-nourished. She did not see the clear blue autumn sky, or the colors of the turning leaves unless they lay under her feet. Seasons no longer meant anything to her, except for the varying of her labor. Now, after a morning's travel, her one thought was of end of day when she would be allowed to put down her pack, and after gathering the wood and water take her rag of blanket to one side in the darkness and lie down. Maybe she would find one of the dogs willing to sleep with her and help her keep warm under the frost.

2

They had started before dawn, in the grey light, when the mist still followed the river. The night before three cannon fired across the Genesee at Gathtsegwarohare announced the arrival of the invading Continental army under General Sullivan, and the Indians knew there was no longer hope for Chenandoanes, the great Seneca Castle. With the first light they had begun to move out along the Buffalo Creek trail toward Niagara. Maybe the British there would give them enough food to keep alive through the winter.

The long line of women under their heavy loads was here and there punctuated by an old man carrying nothing but his blanket, or a brave with his musket, powderhorn, bullet pouch, and knife and hatchet. The men walked erect, their faces like wooden carvings; a few of the braves, who had been serving with Colonel Butler hopelessly all summer hoping to find a way of stopping Sullivan's overwhelming army, still wore their war paint. Their chests and faces, striped and designed in black and white and vermilion and yellow, now seemed to merge with the leaves of the woods, now stood out in abrupt hideousness against the dull grass and the blue sky. Once in a while one would drop out of the line to talk to another and their voices, or the voice of a wayward child complaining of the weight of her minute pack while her mother admonished her, were the only sounds to break the tread of moccasins and the steady squeak of brow straps.

The woman ahead of the slave had a papoose in his baby frame tied to the back of her pack. The smudgy small eyes unwinkingly watched the woman so close to him. He looked like a doll, helpless in his swaddles, with the beaded hood drawn down to shade his face. The few times when a dip or elevation of the trail brought him level with her eyes, he looked exactly the same, his face as expressionless as one of the old men's. It gave no warning when suddenly he decided to do his business, and the abrupt squirt traveled down the creased corn leaf that entered his wrappings, and spattered directly at the slave's feet.

She stopped instinctively. Instantly the heavy voice of the squaw behind commanded her to go on and in the same breath the hickory gad swished and struck her legs full force. She stepped back, caught her heel on the side of the trail, and fell sideways under her load. As she rolled over to get under her load, the squaw struck again, knocking her back. The squaw's face was phlegmatic, unconcerned. Only her eyes heated; and then suddenly the woman on the ground became aware of the increased outpouring of her rank odor. She made a desperate effort, floundered up; the pack, pulling her to one side, lifted her face. With cold deliberation the squaw lashed her full in the face.

Two thick streams of blood burst from the woman's nose. She swayed for an instant, regained her balance, and doggedly took after the squaw ahead. The Indians behind, who had been stolidly waiting, grunted once or twice and resumed the burden of their march.

When the white woman overtook the forward line she saw that the papoose had finished piddling, but his eyes now fixed on her bleeding nose immovably. The instinct for impersonal cruelty was already apparent in his doll-like face. But she did not see it; she saw only the narrow dark trodden slot of the trail, on which the blood dropped slowly to mark her steps.

She stopped bleeding at last, but she was not conscious of it. She moved in a daze containing the weariness and misery of her body, unthinking and unreasoning, until in the afternoon they reached a stopping place. There she was allowed to put down her pack and sent away to gather wood.

A small stream beside the trail flowed through an alder scrub. Through this she blindly found her way, and lying down full length on the bank dipped her face in the water, drinking a little, and clumsily washing off the blood.

Behind her among the Indians camped along the trail an excited ruffle of talk broke out. Suddenly from the way they had come appeared a company of men in green and black dress. They looked worn-out and sick and weary, too; their coats stained from sleeping coverless, their shoes broken through with weeks of wilderness marching. Only their guns and bayonets looked clean and ready for service.

They passed the place where the woman lay and made their own camp farther down the trail. But one of them, coming along the brook to find a place deep enough to fill his kettles, surprised her still lying there. As she struggled to get up, he said, "Don't mind me, Grandma," in a good-natured Irish voice.

At the sound of spoken English, she lifted her head with a quick, startled motion and stared at him. He looked young. He was a tall, rangy fellow with a long upper lip and a blunt tilted nose. He paid no attention to her at first, filling his buckets, but as he rose he met her eyes.

"Jesus," he said. "You're white."

She nodded.

"With them?" he said, tilting his head back towards the Indians.

She nodded again. Her mouth worked and her plain face puckered as she tried to fit her lips to the unfamiliar sounds of English speech. He watched her in a kind of fascination, seeing the sweat come out on her face, until she finally managed a halting articulation: "I've been with them over a year."

It seemed then that he really saw her, her raggedness and the blood, still smeared on her chin, and the scars on her gaunt bare legs.

"They made you into a slave," he said. "I've heard they do it sometimes. The bloody-minded dirty devils."

She shrank back a little, then made a furtive pitiful attempt to draw her dress together. He tactfully looked away and cursed softly.

"Where'd they get you?" he asked in a lowered voice.

"Dygartsbush, in June, last year."

"It's September now," he said, feeling suddenly uncomfortable.

She said, "Yes." He thought her voice sounded like a ghost's, as though the most part of her had died already. "What's your name, ma'am?"

"Martha Dygart." She stared at him with widened eyes and suddenly dropped her face to her hands and began to sob. She made a rough gasping noise of it, not the way most women cried. He looked round nervously. "Hush, hush," he said. "They'll hear. They're feeling ugly now. The rebels was coming down on Chenandoanes when we left there." He cocked his head at her. "Listen, why don't you clear out and get back and meet their army? They'd take you home."

She shook her head.

"Why not?"

"*She'd* find me," she said after a moment.

"She? Who's she?"

"Gekeahsawsa."

He gave it up. He had never got on with Indians.

She lifted her gaunt face.

"Can't I go with you?"

He swore under his breath.

"Please," she said. "I can do hard work. I can cook. I could get wood and cook for a lot of you." Her eyes looked pitiful to him. "They used to say I was a good hand to cook. Even my husband said so."

"Listen, ma'am. Indians are fit to kill any white man now — don't matter which side he's on, just any white man. Butler said for us not to have no truck with them at all."

He felt ashamed to see the way she huddled down, just like a dog a man was misusing.

"I'm just a private," he explained. "I can't do nothing."

She did not look up, but said in a muffled voice: —

"I could sew for you. Mend your things." He saw the blood rise painfully in her cheeks and she looked up suddenly at him. "I know what you're thinking. I can't seem to sew with their big needles. But I used to do fine-sewing when I had my own house." He could hardly hear her voice. "They burned it," she said. "I ain't got anywhere to go."

"God, that's too bad," he said. "Did they kill all your family?"

"Yes. Only my little girls. They was hunting the cow."

"Listen," he said. "If you got back to Sullivan's army they'd take you back to your little girls."

"I guess they're dead," she said. "They was awful little, Lucy was seven and Pearl was five. The Indians killed everybody else in the settlement."

The ranger kept looking round like a man trying to talk his way out of something he hadn't meant to start.

"Niagara ain't no place for you, Mrs. Dygart. It ain't going to be a good place this winter. We'll have the most of the Seneca nation hanging round eating off us and there's generally not enough food to go round anyway. It's cold. It's cold as hell."

She said in a heavy voice: "I guess I know how you feel about the Indians."

She made him feel ashamed. He had never felt so ashamed. Now if she'd been a girl, or pretty, he thought, he could have taken a chance and maybe got the sergeant interested.

"I feel sorry for you, ma'am. Honest to God I do."

She huddled down on the ground like someone with the life all gone out of her. Through her torn dress he could see the way her back was scarred. He got up and stood there doing foolish things with his hands, trying to think of how he could get away. Then a yell down the trail helped him out.

"Burke! Burke! Where the hell is that ugly dumbhead gone to? Hey, Burke!"   —

"That's Sergeant hollering for me, ma'am." He tried to make his voice sound funny. He hadn't expected her to smile, but she did not even lift her head. "I got to get back." He did feel sorry for her; he remembered what she had said about sewing. Fine-sewing. He looked at her hands. Impulsively he reached into his pocket and pulled out a thin fold of black leather which he dropped into her lap.

"It ain't no good to me," he apologized. "But maybe you could use it. Good luck, ma'am."

He went striding off through the grey twilight of the alders, slopping water from both buckets.

3

She heard him going; but she was too tired now even to look after him. She forgot all about the wood she was going to get. Her face hurt her. She knew from other beatings she had had, when Gekeahsawsa had driven her out of the cabin, how the cold could make its own agony in the hurt places of her body. Some of those nights she had slept out with the dogs by the house wall. Sometimes they would let her work into their beds: nights when wolves were running back of the lake they seemed to be glad of her company. But those nights, even when the dogs were good to her, she could feel the cold creep into her sore muscles as plain as if it were a living thing that walked.

Along the trail, fires were beginning to take life from dry bark. The flames caught hold of sticks and sent up curled strings of rusty smoke. The smoke spread out along the line of fires, and then, responding to a slight draft, floated like a moving shelf over the alders.

She could smell it, acrid and half sweet; and her eyes smarted, not so much from the smoke itself as from the memory of winter nights when she had managed to lie forgotten in her corner of the house. On such nights the vent holes in the roof were nearly closed to preserve the warmth, and the smoke became a pall, filling the air, until the papooses hanging inscrutably in their swaddles sud-denly acquired the human animation of coughing. Nobody ever noticed them. Their little coughing voices would go on until the fires died. But often the smoke hung so low that it was hard for the adults on the floor to breathe.

The men would sit together, sometimes playing the peach-stone games, sharpening a knife or hatchet, or splic-ing a snowshoe frame. The women made moccasins and leggings or did beadwork. The dark faces intent upon their employment were now lost in the waving smoke, now apparent, red in the light of the four fires. When the men talked of war trails or long hunts, telling their stories with rolling periods as though the unriddling of an otter's tracks might be compared to the unfolding of the universe, the words sounded as though they passed through a thick gauze. Eyes became infected from the constant irritation and often long before the end of winter persons went half-blind with a constant running from their underlids. Smoke to Martha Dygart would all her life be an Indian thing; smoke and the smell of the head woman of the house.

Once Martha had been made to clean the pelt of a wolverine. The woman's scent was like it, rank and musty, as though she lived on blood, like one of the weasel tribe.

It was nearly dark under the alders when Martha's hand brushed against the fold of leather the ranger had left lying in her lap. She lifted it wonderingly, feeling the tears rise. She did not know why she felt like crying now; she never thought of it. Tears often came when she found herself alone, though she had never been a weepy woman. They were a kind of luxury.

Her calloused, work-stiffened fingers were clumsy, like a child's attempting to open a purse. When she had it open she thought for a moment that there was nothing in it; that he had given it to her merely because it was the only thing he had to give away. But it was nice to have, smelling as it did of white man's leather, a little tobacco-y, a little of sweet oil as if he had spilled a few drops on it once when cleaning his gun, and strangely also a little of green soap. It was the soap smell that made her think of her own cabin, and she had an overwhelming memory of the clean things of her former life — of washdays and of the steaming soapy smell of damp cloth when the iron hissed on it, and of fresh clothes on a line, a whipping wind, a cowbell in the woods, the precise sound of a scythe and stone. She thought suddenly of her children's dresses. She had made them out of a calico that had a violet pattern. Violet was a color the Indians did not use. Her breast ached, and her thoughts dizzily mixed in her blurred mind.

The prick on the end of her little finger startled her. It was as though she were learning to sew again; she remembered her early attempts at stitches, long before she became Nicholas Dygart's second wife and moved to

Dygartsbush. She held the leather up, but she had to turn it until the firelight shone across its surface before she saw the needle.

There was no thread, but there was actually a needle. The light outlined it with a faint coppery sheen. She could see it, the full length of it, except where it was passed through the linen strap. She saw also that there was a pocket for a card of thread, but that was empty.

For a while she was afraid to try to touch the needle, thinking it might become a dream. Then tentatively she touched the eye end. Her fingers were clumsy, she could hardly feel the slimness of it. But finally, with great precaution against dropping it, she worked it free. She sat a while holding it, then lifted it in front of her eyes and faced the firelight. Holding it so, she could see it clearly, but she had to turn it between her fingers to bring the eye into view.

She sat there utterly still. It was a white man's needle, the kind of needle a person could do fine work with. Her lips twitched until she could not stop them and she caught the lower in her teeth. She began to move the needle here and there, catching the light at different angles. She was like a child experimenting with it. She held it at arm's length so that the eye was barely discernible; then she moved it slowly closer, as though in dim light she were trying to thread it. When she held it very close to her own eye she found she could see one fire through it. It seemed strange to be able to see so much through so small an aperture. The whole camping group of Indians was encompassed in the needle's eye.

The fire, the kettle on the stick, the papoose on the baby frame leaned against a pack, the squatting brave in apathetic patience waiting his food. His face was painted all one smear of red with three yellow bands that ran from ear to ear, broken only at the nose which carried a vertical white stripe. The feather in his scalp lock dangled over his ear. The bending woman next him minded the pot and fed the flames, and a couple of silent children, large-eyed, tired with hunger, watched her. A single squaw, thick-set and darker-skinned than the other women, stood on the edge of the trail looking down into the alder bed.

The hand holding the needle wavered; Martha slowly let it sink into her lap but her eyes remained fixed on the squaw. She recognized her, and now she remembered that the Wildcat had ordered her to bring in wood. She started to get on her knees with the abject reaction that had become ingrained from fifteen months' abuse. She was so full of panic that she almost dropped the needle. Not quite. As she felt it slipping from her fingers she tightened them frantically, dropping back to the ground to make sure of it. For an instant all thought of everything abandoned her except the one idea that she must place the needle safely in the little book. She worked it deliberately into the linen strap.

Then at last, after what seemed like hours, she stood up and looked at the fire.

4

When the ranger gave Martha Dygart the needle, he had
no idea of the meaning of the gift. Even when Martha first
pricked her finger on its steel point, she was unaware of
what the needle might do for her. She had no inkling of it
even yet. All she knew was that the needle in this wilderness was far too precious for anyone to lose. Her shoulders
squared jerkily and the hand holding the little book closed
on it tight.

The Wildcat was entering the alders. Martha knew at
once that the squaw was coming to find her; she could tell
by the way she walked, deliberately soft-footed, moving her
head from side to side. As the squaw swung slightly to the
right, directly crossing the firelight, Martha saw that she
was carrying a casse-tête or Indian war club. The hand
holding it twitched up the head and let it swing back again;
but for an instant Martha saw it clear against the fire with
its head carved from a knot, and its tuft of hawk's-breast
feathers dangling from the handle. Martha could imagine
the Wildcat's fury if she should find out about the needle.
In Chenandoanes she had seen an Indian trade seven
beaver pelts for one. The Wildcat would kill Martha
half a dozen times to possess it.

Not since the first week or two of her slavery had
Martha had nerve enough to think of acting on her own
impulse. Now she saw that if the Wildcat found her
where she was there would be no chance of keeping the

needle from her except by throwing it away. But she could not do a thing like that; even her husband, who had been grudging in good words, used to admit she was a frugal person. But if she tried to stand up to the Wildcat so near the campfires, one yell from the squaw would bring the Indians pouring into the bushes.

The Wildcat was now not more than sixty or seventy feet away. She had stopped, standing utterly still, a grey shape in the darkness as the firelight outlined her deerskin skirt, like a predatory beast holding its breath for a mouse's scurry. Martha, whether she imagined it or not, caught faintly the strong musky odor. Her heart beat suddenly, as the heart of a mouse might beat, and the instinct of the hunted creature told her not to move until the squaw moved.

The squaw took a few stealthy steps down the creek, and as she started to move Martha stepped back carefully into the brook. She made no sound. Once she was in the water she slid her feet along the bottom, making no splash. The stream itself, covering the round of a log near by, made a faint sound of water to cover her wading. When she came to the far side, she lifted her feet carefully onto the bank and stood still.

The squaw also had stopped again. For a few moments Martha could not make out which way she was headed. Then, whether from some noise she had heard Martha make, from instinct or dead luck, the squaw began to return along the bank of the stream. She came only a short way, however, before stopping once more. Martha quickly bent down and squeezed her dripping skirt tight to her legs so that there would be no drip from the hem. Her feet and legs were so cold that there was no feeling in them. As she crouched there, bent, the squaw stepped into the water, waded over, and climbed out.

They were now on the same bank, with the stream between them and the campfires. Both looked back at them, watching for a moment the still, blanketed forms of the Indians. The whole line was quietly settling down for the night.

On the side of the stream on which the two women now were the earth was covered with a knee-high stand of grass. Scattered alder bushes made some cover, enough to hide them from each other's sight. But a stand of woods began on the slope beyond the alders, running over a low ridge. Through these, even in the darkness, several coverts of young hemlock made darker blotches. As she faced the higher ground Martha thought that if she could once get into one of these coverts the squaw could never find her in the dark. She would only have to lie still until she heard which way the Indian went, then work her way out the other side, circling if necessary to strike the back trail to Chenandoanes. Her heart beat heavily. It was the first time she had definitely thought of trying to escape. For the first time, also, it seemed possible.

A thin skimming of clouds that had stolen out of the west since sunset obscured the stars. The moon was only a dim glow low over the ridge, seeming to take light rather than give it to the world. The only light in the shallow valley came from the line of campfires. As she glanced back at them, Martha understood why the squaw was heading for the higher ground. It was essential therefore for Martha not to let the squaw get far enough ahead to see her against the firelight.

The Wildcat had already started, moving as quietly as the beast she was named for, as though she had pads on her feet. Now and then Martha was aware of a deeper silence that warned her that the squaw had stopped again, and in such moments she stopped herself and fought to breathe quietly.

Though she moved so slowly it seemed strange that she should breathe so hard. It made her head swim to keep in her mind all the things she had to do. She must feel for dry sticks with her feet, letting down her weight with caution. Doing so she had to be careful of her balance. She had to keep her hands before her lest she blunder into an alder, and in pushing one aside she must first feel the bark to see if it were dead, for dead alders broke easily. She must stay near enough to the squaw to know where she was going, but she must not get so close that in case she made a sound herself, the squaw could tell where she was.

Once for a moment she lost the Indian, then she heard her break a stick. The sound was like a report, light as it was, and so close that Martha pressed her hands to her breast as if to muffle the sounding of her heart. She waited until the squaw had moved well ahead this time; too far ahead, she realized when it was too late. She had then to strike off at an angle to take cover of the first hemlocks. She bent far over, with her hands almost touching the grass. When she reached the hemlocks she let herself down under them and lay panting.

She could no longer hear the squaw at all. She had no longer any way of knowing whether the squaw were ahead of her or not, and her original plan of waiting until she could take a line of her own had become impossible. It occurred to her that if the squaw could not find her soon, she would return and get the men out on a search.

Martha lay still, wondering what she should do. But instead of making plans all her tired brain could think of were the endless miseries the Wildcat had put upon her: the useless beatings, when her slowness was due merely to her lack of understanding of the language; the overloading on the march; the skimping of her food when other prisoners were allowed to share the best; the inexplicable outbursts of sheer fury. The woman had a natural instinct for evil. But above all it was the glittering pleasure in the small black eyes that Martha kept thinking of when the Wildcat used to drive her out of the lodge on winter nights.

Martha rose instinctively and, putting aside the hemlock branches with her hands, worked clear of their shelter. She paused on the edge of the covert, listening; then in the silence moved slowly further into the woods. No longer attempting to move quietly, she took a natural pace. But whenever her feet encountered a stick on the ground she picked it up. She tried several before she found one of a length and strength that seemed to suit her, and after that she payed no attention to anything but the night around her.

She knew that the Wildcat would find her soon enough. Her heart worked with regular but heavy beats. She was not afraid that the squaw might yell. Let her yell. She would deal with her before the men could come, for she realized now that her months of heavy labor had strengthened her muscles. She might not have as much endurance, owing to her scant feeding, but she had strength enough to deal with any other woman.

As she walked, her mind became exalted. She felt herself to be an avenging justice, as though the circumstances of all her life had been ordained to bring this one moment to pass. Then, as she came to the top of the ridge, and saw the dim glow of the moon through clouds once more, she knew that the squaw was near, and she stood still waiting.

The squaw also had stopped, and there was nothing to tell Martha where she stood except the musky exhalation from the Indian's body.

5

It was rank in the damp air. It seemed to come from all sides at once, surrounding Martha with the loathing and fear of past months. But she no longer wanted to escape.

The squaw's voice came abruptly out of the darkness.

"Where is the wood?"

Martha stood still, drawing her breath silently.

"You have not got it. I told you to bring wood."

Martha did not even move her head, but her eyes kept searching the darkness inch by inch.

"I have seen you coming." The harsh voice sounded almost patient. "You go back now."

For a moment Martha thought, *By the hemlock. It's about her height.*

"I know where you stand, white woman."

That's a lie, she thought. It wasn't by the hemlock. She heard a light rustle of leaves. The squaw was still now, too. Both women listened to it. Martha moved a quick pace to face the sound — then realized that the squaw had moved too. And both of them stood still.

"Answer me."

If I could only see her. A slight rising of damp air from the valley behind them brought the sound of an Indian speaking; then a cry went down the line of fires. The Rebel army was in Chenandoanes.

"Go back now," commanded the heavy voice.

I'm not going back. And you aren't either, so help me God.

"I will not beat you very hard. Go back now. If you do not go back I will kill you."

She doesn't know where I am, Martha thought. *She's getting scared, or she wouldn't say that.*

A faint whisper of feathers passed close over their heads. Martha looked quickly up and saw the long wing of an owl float across the cloudy gleam of the moon. Then he was gone as though absorbed by the night and the woods. But a moment later, as Martha tried desperately to think, his maniacal screech rang over the dark woods. In the appalling hush that followed, she caught her breath. *That black lump beside the trunk of the second beech tree. It had moved.*

"You thought you could get away. But the Wildcat sees in the dark." The voice became grim. "She has long claws."

Two long steps. If she were only sure. Martha's gaunt face was working childishly in the darkness. *I can't stand it any more.*

"You did not get far, white woman."

Martha drew her breath.

"A ranger gave me a needle, Gekeahsawsa," she said aloud. "I have it in my hand. It is a steel needle."

She stepped quickly one long pace down the ridge.

"Give it to me."

Now she was sure. The voice had moved too. Now she could tell where it came from. She turned herself with infinite slowness. "You can have it, Gekeahsawsa." *Come and get it now.* She raised her stick, waiting, suddenly counting her own heartbeats.

"Bring it to me."

The squaw had moved again. Now Martha heard her, a small stick breaking halfway through and leaves pressed down. The squaw's odor was a sudden rank outpouring. *I'm not afraid.* She heard the swish of the casse-tête almost too late and threw herself to one side. The ironwood burl cracked against the tree she had been hugging, glanced, bounced off her left shoulder. The pain did not stun her. From her knees she struck out with all her might, knee-high, and felt it hit home. The squaw grunted as her feet gave way. She floundered backward into the brush and went down with a crash. A half-articulate shout rose in Martha as she hurled her broken stick at the crashing in the bushes and rushed after it herself.

6

It was pitch-dark in the thicket of witch's hobble. When the squaw, still on her back, struck upward at Martha, the long stems snared the head of the casse-tête, and the blow served only to tell Martha where the Indian lay. She felt the blow in the bushes against her face and threw herself full length onto the struggling squaw.

The Wildcat had dropped the club and her hands met Martha's. She yanked her down on top of herself and caught her hair with one hand while the other clawed at Martha's face. A wave of nausea shook the white woman as she felt the nails rake through her skin. She had a sudden insane vision of the hand, the seamed knuckles, the hard brown skin, and the heavy, blunt-ended nails ragged and dirty. She threw herself to one side to dodge them and instantly the squaw's thick body bounced over against her, throwing her flat.

They rose unsteadily together. "Go back now . . ." the voice began triumphantly. Martha struck at it with her clenched fist and felt the woman's eye against her knuckles. The squaw gave a yelp of furious surprise, caught her arm and yanked her close. Martha gave with the pull, then when she was close broke free of the squaw's grip and threw her arms around the heavy body. She was surprised how easy it had been to break the squaw's hold. She fumbled now with her feet to trip her, but it was a clumsy business with both of them in skirts, and they rocked and pitched on the sloping ground, with the witch's hobble threshing into their faces. Martha felt her own hair in front of her eyes, but eyesight did not count. She worked around the squaw until she was uphill of her and then put forth all her strength to throw her.

For a few moments the squaw resisted. Then without warning she made a frenzied attempt to break away. She was frightened at last; Martha recognized the fact with a fierce thrill. The very effort of the Wildcat to get away defeated her for she lost balance. She went over backwards down the slope of the ground with Martha on top.

Martha sensed the yell before it was born. She shifted with her hands and found the thick neck and pressed her thumbs over the throat with all her might. The first wild screech was shut off in a bubbly gasp; it was like the spitting of a cat. Martha could feel the muscles under her thumbs strain with the effort to yell. *Try and yell now!* But the squaw had already given up trying to yell and was struggling to draw breath. Martha felt the labored breathing of the thick chest beneath her as the hands tore at her wrists. *I won't let go.* The squaw's body scent became a stench. The thick legs kicked, the moccasined heels drumming on the ground. Her hands left Martha's wrists to tear at her breast and grope over her face.

Two fingers thrust suddenly into Martha's nostrils and the thumb forced between her lips. She jerked her head, but the fingers did not let go. She felt as if her whole face were being torn. Without letting go the neck, she hoisted herself and brought one knee down on the squaw's abdomen, grinding it in with all the power she had. The thick body flopped convulsively, and wrenched away beyond her strength to hold. The squaw rolled free.

By the same impetus Martha was flung back. She felt a hard knob under her side and instinctively put her hand down to relieve the pressure. Her fingers closed on the handle of the club. She struggled up, panting and trembling, with the thing in her hands. A little way down the slope the rolling flurry of leaves and sticks stopped with a sudden thud.

Martha listened a moment, but she heard no sound. She wiped her face with her free hand, pushed back her hair, and then began to descend to where the sound had stopped. She went as quickly as she could in the dark; but at every other step she paused, straining her ears to listen. She knew the squaw must be lying utterly still, trying to find breath to yell with; and she knew that above all she must get to her before she yelled.

Then just below her feet, she detected the thin wheezing of the efforts to breathe. She knelt, hoping to raise the other's body against the faint sheen of moonlight. At first she saw only the silhouette of a little hemlock tree, then the three fronds of a brake. It seemed to her that the Wildcat must be unaware of how close she was. Perhaps she had been partly stunned. She waited patiently, with a thin smile, for the other to rise, and her fingers, that ached from clenching the thick throat, wrapped themselves round the handle of the casse-tête.

The Wildcat stirred. Her breathing, which had lost its whistling note, still rasped painfully. She was like a wounded beast lifting herself on her hands in the darkness and drawing her feet under her one after the other. An ecstatic sense of power invaded Martha. She waited until the Indian was standing before she rose herself.

Now she could see the round of the head outlined, round as the knob of the casse-tête.

"Look," she said. "I am here."

The squaw turned stupidly and as she did Martha swung the casse-tête.

It was as if the balance of the weapon guided it home. The sound on the skull was like a splitting pumpkin. The squaw fell; it seemed as if she crumpled on herself, and Martha, watching her, knew at once that she was dead.

Her own legs gave way. She sat helplessly clenching the handle of the casse-tête. It had not seemed like a heavy blow at all. A faint wonder came over her. She reached out her free hand and felt the inert lump of clothes and body on the leaves like a crumpled toadstool. There was no motion, no sound.

She sat there for a long time before she stirred; but in that time she had once a queer frightening sense of the woman's musky odor rising even after death. It seemed to make a cloud in the damp air hanging about them both until, mysteriously, it was gone as if it had floated off with ghostly stealth among the tree trunks.

Her laughter was a frightening sound to hear in the dark woods. After a while, Martha herself heard it; but as soon as she heard it the sound ceased. Then she rose to her feet and walked a little way back up the slope. She halted suddenly. She was motionless for a minute.

She had remembered the needle. She knew that it was

lost. She had no light nor way of making light. Her lips quivered. She began to weep. She went for a long roundabout search, but she could not find the broken witch's hobble.

7

Several times after sunrise she dropped flat in the brakes to watch small parties of Indians trotting past along the trail. They went by without glancing right or left. There was something frightened in the blind way they ran, as if all they wanted was to overtake the main body of Indians.

She did not see any white rangers with them either; and after eleven o'clock she met no one at all. The feeling that she was all alone came over her. She had no notion of the landmarks and no way of telling how far she was from Chenandoanes.

But towards noon she noticed a tower of smoke to the east and she knew that she must be getting near. Even then she was careful to stay away from the trail.

The smoke rose over the tops of the trees and billowed slightly towards the southeast. As she approached she could see in it fountains of sparks bursting upward to immense heights. And suddenly she was on the highland west of the river and had a full view of the valley.

The first thing that met her eyes was a wide swathe beaten through the high grass like a road; then as she came out upon the brow of the slope she saw the town. All the houses were blazing. The leaping flames looked dull compared to the maple trees and the smoke was rusty against the clear sky.

Off to the south of the town several small tents were pitched and before these, from a lance planted in the ground, hung a bright-colored flag. She stared at it, never having seen it before, and she thought that it was prettier with its red and white stripes than any militia flag she had ever seen. It looked so clean and fresh, and she had the notion even at that distance that it had been made of silk. Involuntarily her hands strayed over her breast, pulling together the shredded remnants of her overdress.

When she looked down she could see men everywhere throughout the town. They swarmed among the houses like blue-coated ants. A great company of them was in the cornfield cutting down the corn like harvesters. They did not pull the ears; they cut the drying stalks and a long double line of them extended all the way to the blazing houses to pitch the stalks onto the blaze. Every bundle sent up a burst of sparks, and these were like fountains playing regularly through the town.

Over the whole scene a continual play of sound was audible, punctuated by the ring of rangers' axes in the apple orchards. At first it sounded strange to Martha, then she realized that it was the sound of thousands of voices speaking English.

Suddenly she was afraid to go down among them with her scratched face and matted hair and tattered clothes. She felt naked and dirty and indecent. Her throat started to work and she began to sob tearlessly.

She sat down, trying to muster courage, and watched

the swift disappearance of the standing corn into the burning houses. She must have sat there nearly an hour before
she saw several figures emerge from the tents south of the
town. They looked spruce and bright in their blue coats
and buff breeches. A thin piercing silvery note of a whistle
lifted above the roar of destruction and a few moments
later some soldiers led horses to the tents.

Martha had not seen a horse for months. The sight of
them electrified her. As the men mounted she rose with
the same motion. They rode directly towards her, making
a circuit of the blazing town.

When they were under her, the leader made a gesture
with his hands and a man behind him lifted a bugle to
his lips. The shining notes rang over all the valley, seeming
to make the air bright. Other bugles caught the notes and
echoed them here and there; and then a roll of drums beat
the muster.

Everywhere the men stopped and went to their rifles.
Platoons started forming and marched away towards the
tents. The destruction was over. Chenandoanes would
never exist again.

Martha moved hesitantly down. A corporal saw her
coming and broke out of his platoon. It seemed to her
that half the army turned to look at her. She hung back,
trying to cover her nakedness.

The corporal came towards her.

"You're white," he said.

"Yes, my name's Martha Dygart."

"You was a prisoner?"

"Yes."

His sunburned face looked kind. "Here, ma'am," he said, and took off his coat and helped her put it on. "The General will want to talk to you."

She was led through the entire army. When she came out at the head, she saw the General standing beside his horse, and men behind him taking down the small tent. She realized all at once that the men looked ragged and that even the General's coat was stained.

He took off his hat to her, baring a red thatch of hair, and smiled briefly.

The corporal saluted and explained, "An Indian captive just come in, sir."

"You just got here in time," the General said. "We are starting our return march in twenty minutes."

He pulled out a large silver watch as though to verify himself. Then suddenly he asked her questions.

What was her name? Where did she come from? Where had the Indians escaped? Where was Colonel Butler? How far was it to Niagara? How far had the Indians gone to the west?

She tried to answer them as well as she could, but she could see that he thought her stupid and her information worthless.

"Very well, ma'am," he said. "I'll put you under Dr. Minema's care. He's surgeon of the First New York. They come from your section, I believe." He turned. "Dr. Minema, will you look out for this poor woman?"

"Yes, General Sullivan."

That was all. The doctor led her away. He pulled a piece of loaf sugar from his knapsack and gave it to her.

"You look as if you needed food. We'll be able to give you something more tonight. There's no time now."

Martha said "Thank you," dully. She heard the drums rolling and the sound went over the wide valley. Behind the mustered columns the smoke of Chenandoanes rolled upward, leaning in the wide sky. Then the army started to move with a sudden jolting of cannon, click of bullet pouches, and stamp of feet. It seemed to her a greater sound than the roll of drums.

She walked heavily behind the doctor, her gaunt face lost in thought. She knew she was slow-witted, but the rising smoke reminded her of her two children and her own burning cabin. And she thought if only twenty of these five thousand men had been placed under arms at Dygartsbush the Indians never would have dared attack it. She would have liked, too, to tell the red-haired Irish General that Albany was quite a ways from the Little Lakes where Dygartsbush was. She would have thought that having come so far he might have realized that some places were pretty far apart.

"Why don't you eat the sugar?" the doctor asked.

Dumbly she put it in her mouth; and after that for more than a mile all she could think of was how long it was since she had tasted sugar.

ELLEN MITCHEL

THE two children taken captive in the raid on Dygartsbush
got over their fear of the Indians almost at once. The boy,
Peter Kelly, was over thirteen; Ellen Mitchel was a month
or two younger. They were of an age to forget what they
had seen of the raid, and indeed, in Ellen's case, that was
little enough. She had gone out to look for the cow, got
twisted in the darkness, and lost her way in the woods.
She could hear the shooting, the wild high-pitched yells of
the Indians, and see the glow of burning cabins through
the trees or the glow of the fire against the rainy sky, but
instinct had kept her in the woods. She was crouched there
on the edge of a clump of bushes when Skanasunk, the
Fox, came along hauling Peter Kelly behind him.

He was a great strapping young brave. Often in the years
following she was to remember him as he stepped round
the bushes. A high leap of the fire gave her a clear glimpse
of him against the trees, all coppery and shining with the
rain; the bear on his chest painted in black; the upper
part of his face painted red and his cheeks black with white
stripes on them. He had a feather in his scalp lock and a
beaded deerskin breechcloth that hung down before and
behind. (She hadn't been able to see then just how it was
put on; but she found out later that it was passed between
the legs and held in place by a thong around the belly.)
He looked long-legged and swift; but even then, seeing him
in the firelight under the dripping branches, she did not

think he looked ugly, just hideous and wild and fierce. She liked those things and she liked the feeling that she belonged to him, especially when she saw the other Indians and the way they abused the women in the line of captives. She did not know that her own family had been wiped out; she thought, when she thought at all about it, that her mother must be with another band of the Indians. She enjoyed the camping at night and the feeling of privilege she and Pete had in not being tied down. Skanasunk seemed to enjoy letting them have the run of the camp; and after supper they were allowed to sleep near the fire alongside of him.

Before the Indians tomahawked her, old Mrs. Staats had tried to put a stop to Ellen's familiarity with the Indians. It was bad enough, she said, for Ellen to be running around with a good-for-nothing limb of the woods like Peter Kelly; but it would have made her mother fit to die if she could have seen Ellen sleeping right next to a half-naked savage. Ellen was thirteen now, Mrs. Staats pointed out to her uninterested companions; the girl was getting to be womanish.

Ellen had a brief moment of horror the night Mrs. Staats was killed. Seeing Mrs. Staats's scalp dried and stretched and hooped was somehow different, it having all happened right in front of her. It made her serious and for several days she kept tight to Pete, so close that he became embarrassed and spoke of her scornfully, calling her a sissy-girl. But she accepted his taunts meekly and stuck to him like a leech; and she noticed that even Pete was inclined to stay as near to Skanasunk as possible. On the night after, he went so far as to admit that he was glad it was Skanasunk who had taken them both.

"Why?" she asked, though she echoed him in her heart.

"Aren't you too?" he demanded. "He don't look so full of poison."

"No," she said. It was true. He treated them different; he was always ready to show her how he painted the bear on his chest; he acted proud of it, though she felt she could paint one that would look a whole lot more like a bear. But for her the real reason for being glad was the feeling that she and Pete would be together.

Skanasunk confirmed this the evening after he left the main band on the headwaters of the Chemung. While they all three hunched round their small fire that evening to watch the thin naked body of a hare give way in the boiling water, he took them into his confidence. He even smiled at them, a broad and big-toothed grin through his worn paint. He said he was going to adopt them both. That is, he would get his wife to adopt them. Women, he explained, did adopting in the Indian nations. She was a fine squaw, he said, and she had lost one child by her first husband and another child by him, which made her feel sad. Now that he had two healthy children for her, she would feel better. It would be fine having two healthy children in his house. It made him feel good himself to think of it. They would like it in the Indian village. Pete would not have to work and Ellen could learn cooking and making skins soft under his wife's guidance.

"Shucks," said Pete. "I never was a hand to work. But I'm good at hunting."

"Teach you hunt," said Skanasunk. "Some time pretty soon you big man, I buy you gun maybe. Fine gun like mine."

2

The name of the village was Tecarnohs. It was a small place of half a dozen houses and perhaps ten families and the council house was no more than a small bark cabin in the open land by the bend of the creek. They came overland to it from the Genesee watershed, keeping a small trail above the rough creek beds, and looked down at it from one of the steep hills late in the afternoon.

Only a couple of the houses could be seen. For the most part they were scattered here and there through the woods wherever the ground served. It was not a close community; and many of the dwelling houses were of bark.

The creek wound down through the narrow valley, catching a sheen from the sunlight where the woods did not shadow it. It had the look of good fishing water, and Pete said, "It appears good country to me," soberly, as his small face turned north and south, and his eyes took in the rough hills and heavy woods.

Skanasunk grunted and stretched a bare arm upstream, to point out a small house. "My house," he said. "Corn patch there. Have garden back of house." He touched Ellen's shoulder with the ball of his thumb. "See Newataquaah."

Looking down, Ellen made out the foreshortened figure

of an Indian woman before the entrance of the house. She was dressed in deerskins and she was at the moment bending over a stump mortar to grind corn. Her brown hands worked the pestle steadily and a faint sound of it came up to them, *tap, tap, tap,* as soft as though it were the tail of the bitch patting the dust in the sunlight close by while a mess of puppies suckled her like wrestlers. Ellen glanced quickly at Skanasunk, but he was not looking at her, but over the valley. He had refreshed his paint that morning after oiling himself. His feather made a moving bar of shadow over one shoulder as it moved in the wind. It was hard to think of him as having feelings when you looked at him, and yet she felt that he had pointed out his squaw so she would have an interest in the town. It wasn't the kind of thing you expected of an Indian, but she felt sure of it, and her thin brown face softened.

She did not know what was getting into her lately, the way she was feeling soft about people, about places, even about the woods. She could see a hawk fly in a bright sky and feel herself go all warm inside. She knew what Pete would say if she told him about it — he would say she was getting notional; and she did not want Pete to think of her as a notional woman. Notional women sometimes had a hard time marrying unless they had money. She would never have money herself, though there were wealthy Mitchel people, she had heard, back in Cherry Valley. She gave herself a pinch on her thigh, squeezing her fingers until they hurt, and made herself think reasonably. It was hard to tell what a person was like, she thought, seeing them from as far as she saw Skanasunk's squaw.

Ellen could not see herself, of course. She hardly ever thought of what she looked like. She still had the lanky figure of a girl, with long flat legs that were more likely to break out running than to carry her at a nice walk. Her petticoat, grown ragged from her long journey, showed her ankles scarred and scratched, and the feet bruised, like any little girl's. But there was a suggestion of what Mrs. Staats had called her "growing womanish" in the slight rounding under her blue and white shortgown. Except for that shortgown she looked all brown, almost a nut brown; brown hair, brown eyes, and a clear, tanned, unfreckled skin.

As he glanced at her, Pete's thoughts veered irrationally from a vision of a twelve-point buck. She looked kind of pretty, he thought; she had curly hair that showed even with the braids. Both started as Skanasunk cupped his mouth in his hands and let out a high-pitched wavering cry.

Instantly the bitch jumped to her feet, shaking off puppies right and left, and the squaw's hands stopped on the pestle. The barking of dogs broke out here and there along the creek. A couple of old men who had been smoking together in front of a house got up and shaded their eyes. Skanasunk said, "You come now," and started down the hill at an abrupt trot. The two children were hard put to it to keep pace with him.

Later that summer it seemed odd to think that she had been nervous about meeting Newataquaah. She was a small, neat, birdlike woman, not at all like the person Ellen had visualized from Skanasunk's description. Though she was ten years older than her husband, she was neither wrinkled nor bent. As Ellen came to know her better, she even began to think of her as pretty, much prettier than her own mother had been. There was no fear hanging over Newataquaah's life. And though she performed an immense amount of labor in a day, the work never seemed to oppress her and she found time for everything. As soon as she saw Skanasunk or Pete returning from a morning hunt, she would leave her garden patch or cornfield or stop working her skins to start the pot boiling and give them food. It was a thing every woman was expected to do. She did not ask a man if he wanted food when he entered her house; she had the food itself ready for him. She delighted in making men eat.

With Ellen she showed infinite patience. "You are my own daughter now," she would say. "I would have you sew well. You must learn beadwork. All men value a fine beadworker, and a woman who tends her house. It is so everywhere." She had a slight sidelong smile that made her black eyes shine. When Skanasunk praised some of her own handiwork, she would look down and be silent with pleasure for half a day. Ellen, who liked to work, found the life pleasant. She learned that the Indian women did the labor, not because the men made slaves of them as white people supposed, but because they preferred it so. She also learned that hunting was more arduous than it seemed. A man might be out two days with only a piece of quitcheraw to eat before he brought in meat enough to please his wife. "Let them rest now in summer," said Newataquaah. "It is their easy time while we lay up our winter's corn. When the cold comes, then women sit inside by the fire and the men must hunt in the snow."

The only thing that seemed strange to Ellen was how a man so young as Skanasunk could be happy with an older wife. When a woman married a man younger than herself in the settlements back home, people shook their heads and said, "Give Mabel two years afore John commences looking round," the way they spoke of the Franks. But the Indians appeared to take it for granted; and one day when they were working a deerhide together on the fleshing frame, Newataquaah explained to Ellen: "Tecarnohs is a little village and far off from the big trails. But it is good hunting country and we have enough to eat and we do not see many white traders so there are not many drunken people. We are able to keep the old ways. My first husband was an old man. I married him when I was fourteen years old. He died after a while; he was a wise man. Then Skanasunk's mother wished him to marry me. He is a young man. From my first husband I learned how to be wise. When I die Skanasunk will have had time to find his wisdom. Then if he likes he will marry a young girl. So we are not unhappy." She gave Ellen her sidelong smile. "But now we have children. We are both very happy now."

Ellen said impulsively, "I am happy too."

3

Peter Kelly, of course, was in his natural element, without any of his brothers or his drunken old father to order him around. Not that they ever tried to get him to work — they hardly did a lick themselves. But in Tecarnohs a man was meant to hunt and fish, and trap enough to get a couple of bales every year or two to trade for beads, an iron kettle, a gun, or a knife. He lorded it over the Indian lads for even those who were larger than he were not permitted to go out with a gun, and it soon was made evident that Pete was far and away the best shot in the village. Skanasunk made no bones about it, but went around making boasts of his son's prowess. "It's a queer thing," Peter said one evening to Ellen. "Old Skanasunk, he really does think I'm his son. He told me about his son and periently if he was alive he'd be four years old now. But I got his name and it don't make no difference — I just am, the way his heathen mind looks at it. My name's Deawendote. Know what that means? Constant Dawn. Don't they have the craziest ideas? It's the same way with Newataquaah — I bet she figures you're her genuine daughter, the one she had by her first man."

"Yes, she does," Ellen said.

"It's kind of a nuisance, you know," Pete said.

"What do you mean?"

Pete was at work swabbing out the musket. His small dark face was intent upon his job and when he answered

her he used his offhand voice. "Why," he said, "I was talking to Skanasunk about it. I said to him, I said, 'If you
really think we're your own children,' I said, 'how are me
and Ellen going to get married?'"

Ellen raised her eyes from the legging seam she was
stitching with sinew. "You and me marry!"

He had given her one quick look.

"Sure," he said. "You want to stay here, don't you? I
mean when are you and me going to get away? White
people don't come this way. Why, we might have to stay
here four, five years."

"I hadn't thought," she confessed. "But we don't need
to get married about it."

Pete crossed his legs. "Do as you're a mind to," he
said. "I ain't going to bother you. I can get along with one
of them little Indian girls. Some of them are really pretty
and no browner than you be. I just thought it'd save you
marrying an Indian."

Ellen gasped and stared at him.

"I don't think I'd want to marry an Indian."

Pete nodded.

"That's it — but how can you and me marry if we're
brother and sister this way? That's what I said to Skanasunk. First he said we was both too young, but I said no,
you was about eighteen now and I was only four so we'd
be doing what him and Newataquaah had done. Then I
told him your real Ma wanted you to marry me before we
turned into Indians."

"You know that's not so, Peter Kelly."

"Well, I bet she'd rather have you marry even me than a

greasy Indian. Anyhow I told him. And he said he'd have to look it up with the Honundeont, whoever she is. Kind of a she-preacher, maybe. She lives down on the Genesee somewhere. This town ain't got one, not big enough, and he won't see her for a while, probably." He laid the gun aside and grinned. "Poor old Skanasunk, he's so mixed up with what we're his children and Newataquaah's, and being two white people which he doesn't want to admit but knows is so, and how old we are one way and how old the other, he's fit to scratch the back of his ear with his hind leg. But just the same, White-Blanket, I wouldn't mind marrying you."

Ellen flushed. She felt the flush inside her overdress, all over her. She didn't see why she should feel so hot about plain nonsense.

"I guess I've got something to say about that, Master Smart!"

She lifted her chin at him; but he just grinned at her flushed face.

"Oh no, you haven't. You're just a squaw, or you will be when you marry me. And squaws don't never marry with their menfolks, either. Just remember that."

He slid off the sleeping platform and strutted out of the house with his stomach stuck out like a satisfied wiseman's, leaving her alone; and all she could think of was that pretty soon his hair would be long enough to braid. Then in his deerskins he would look like an Indian himself.

4

Tecarnohs was a peaceful place. No war parties passed through it, for it lay between the large towns of the Genesee from which war parties always headed against the Mohawk Valley settlements, and those on the Alleghany whose young braves preferred to strike south. Newataquaah, like the other women, harvested a fair crop of corn and vegetables against the winter and the hunting continued better than usual. Skanasunk had a theory that the constant traveling in other sections of the country was forcing the deer into their own steep valleys.

Towards the middle of October, Skanasunk and Peter, with most of the younger men, struck off down Oil Creek, heading for the Alleghany, which they called the Oheeyo, and the Ohio lands. For a week beforehand, Newataquaah kept herself and Ellen busy pressing parched corn and maple sugar into cakes of quitcheraw, and dicing smoked deer meat and dried blueberries into pemmican. Extra moccasins had to be made, new brow straps braided from elm fibres, leggings and hunting blouses patched. Ellen made Peter secretly a coonskin cap. She thought he was not used to going bareheaded in cold weather, and shaping it for him made her experience a queer sense of motherliness, as if he were a boy she had to look out for. Both of them turned bright red when she presented it the night before they left.

He tried it on in the house; and Newataquaah admired

it. Skanasunk said, "Fine white-man hat"; but when the squaw wanted to sit up all night to make one too, he said no, he was an Indian. It made Pete act sheepish; but he wore it away in the morning, which happened to be a warm one, and Ellen was content. She and Newataquaah had a quiet two months after the men left, during which they made clothes and visited the women in the other houses and spent half of each day bringing dry wood down off the hills.

The snow mounted quickly in their steep valley, once it began to fall, and soon the village was snowed deep in, and the roofs of the houses looked like canoes bottom up upon the crust. The houses themselves became warm and snug. They were laced together by snowshoe trails. Snowshoes were made for the little children so that they might learn, and Ellen, using them daily, learned why the mothers taught their children to toe in.

The men returned from their hunting in early December. They came in just ahead of the first real blizzard, their packs and clothes white and stiff with the driven icy flakes. They had had fair luck and got plenty of beaver and had killed three deer in a small yard on the way back.

At the single-family house of Skanasunk, Newataquaah's eyes sparkled. "Now we will have fresh meat to cook for our two men," she cried to Ellen, and went laughing about her work. Ellen herself had not realized how long they had been without fresh meat. While the men were away all the women had eaten lightly, conserving every bit of smoked meat and their dried berries and squash. But the heaped pots Newataquaah brought out were like a New Year's feast. Skanasunk and Pete gorged themselves until they had to sleep. While they slept the woman and the girl went through their packs, exclaiming at the worn-out moccasins and the mending to be done and showing each other the best pelts. It was a happy time. But Ellen was troubled because she could not find Peter's coonskin cap. She asked him about it next day and he explained readily how it had fallen off when he slipped crossing a brook on a frozen log. He had tried to fish it out with a pole, but the high water sucked it under. Though he sounded contrite, he looked sheepish, and she knew he was lying to her. She said nothing. She had noticed when he first came in that he had braided his hair. It made a queer outlandish tuft on the top of his narrow head. She decided that if they lived to be ninety years apiece she would never make him another.

The winter passed and spring came with a rush and a white frothing of wild cherry on the hills, while the roar of the creek was a voice that filled the valley day after day. In May Newataquaah began to watch the growing moon. The day before it filled she took Ellen to the garden patch and planted her corn and beans in regular spaced hills, five seeds of each, and in the land between the hills she planted squash — the yellow crane-neck squash, and the green round squash, and scalloped squash, the pumpkin, and sunflowers. Then every day she visited the patch, watching first the white lobes of the beans, and then the green pencils of the rolled corn leaves pierce the earth.

That day she made a scarecrow out of an old blouse

and leggings of Skanasunk's, fashioning a ball of bear-skin for the head and fastening a feather to it; and that night she roused Ellen stealthily and beckoned her out to make with her the woman's circle of the crop. Ellen went from curiosity; but the darkness of a starless night filled her with a sense of magic. Newataquaah's hard thin hand with the warm pads on the fingers grasped her own to lead her. They went without light, letting the narrow, hard-worn path direct their feet. A little way from the field Newataquaah stopped and turned to Ellen, placing her finger on her lips first, to silence her. Ellen nodded.

Then she felt the hands lift her overdress up over her shoulders and unknot the skirt thong. A moment later Newataquaah herself undressed. Then she took hands with Ellen again and led the way to the cornfield. Once there, she let go.

Dragging their clothes along the ground behind them, they made the circuit of the planted ground two or three times, by the power of their garments, yet warm from their bodies, drawing a ring around the field that would keep off the cutworm, the wireworm that ate the corn roots, the caterpillar and the grasshopper, and insure the fruitfulness of the crop. It was a strange mysterious business to Ellen. Newataquaah had unbraided her hair and let it hang in a loose invisible cloud upon her shoulders. Clouds covered the stars. One could see only a darker shadow of surrounding woods against an inky sky. Peepers along the creek with voices clear above the sound of water piped with their eternal unconcern; but the woman and the girl went silently, feeling the cold dewy earth between their toes. Once as Ellen, overtaking Newataquaah at a corner of the field, brushed her shoulder against the cool bare skin of the squaw, she was invaded through the touch by a sensation of the power in her body; and when they stole back into the lodge so quietly that even the dogs were not disturbed, she felt herself mysteriously grown. And long after, she lay awake, listening to the creek, and the peepers, and hearing Peter's even breathing.

5

But that summer they became aware of the war. Without warning the Indians from the Alleghany villages passed by Tecarnohs. They came and went in a day, stopping only to be fed. Skanasunk with the men of the village held a long council during the afternoon, and once Peter came back to the house to talk to Ellen.

"There's two armies coming," he said. "One's coming up the Alleghany and the other's coming from Tioga." His face was moody and he acted restless. He stared a moment into Ellen's puzzled face. "Maybe we ought to clear out."

"Clear out?" she echoed.

"Yes. We're white. The armies are burning the towns. Maybe the Indians here won't like us so well now."

"Oh," she said. "But Skanasunk and Newataquaah wouldn't do anything to us."

"They ain't the only Indians." He looked at her again. "Don't you want to go home?"

Ellen looked back at him and suddenly shook her head.

"Me neither," he said. "I like it here."

"So do I, Pete."

He dug the ground with his toe. "Here I'm as good as anybody. They think I'm better than most. I am, too. Back home, I'm just a Kelly. Everybody but Honus is killed."

She had nothing to say. But she heard his voice tighten.

"Back home you wouldn't want to see me any more."

"I would too." She blushed, but her brown eyes met his.

"It wouldn't matter," he said. "They wouldn't let you."

Her thin hands made fists.

"I don't think they'd do anything to us. Let's stay."

"I can't let anything happen to you. I got to look out for you."

"Silly," she said. "They won't hurt me."

He seemed suddenly relieved.

"I'll go back and hang around the council house and see what's going on. But you stay where I can find you."

She promised, and watched him trot away. He did not return till nearly dark. Then he came with Skanasunk.

Skanasunk was serious. "Most people want to go to Niagara, anyway to Chenandoanes," he said to them. "I do not want to go. I do not think the white army will find our little town. Newataquaah does not want to go. We think Niagara is a bad place for our children. The British would find them and make them white again. We do not want them to be white."

Newataquaah shook her head vigorously.

"Even if all the others leave Tecarnohs," continued Skanasunk, "we can live here. *Hano!*"

He stared round solemnly on all three of them; his big nose, black shiny eyes, and flat cheeks like an exaggerated bird's head in the firelight. Way off a dog was barking, shrill as a fox. For a moment they were silent, listening; then Newataquaah's soft voice unexpectedly broke in: "Maybe our children wish to be white again."

It was the first time Ellen had ever seen Skanasunk show surprise. He jerked back his head and looked down his nose at Newataquaah as though her action in speaking were an utterly indecent thing. "A woman has spoken," he began; then he turned his eyes solemnly at the children. "It is so," he admitted. "They have not said."

He looked so completely taken aback, so upset, and so troubled that Ellen felt like crying out, "No, no!" But she drew her breath and looked down modestly at the toes of her moccasins and left it for Pete to answer.

Pete said, "We both of us like it here. We talked about it this afternoon. But maybe some of the other people won't like us now. Maybe we ought to get out before they get mad at us."

Skanasunk beamed all over and Newataquaah with a happy laugh caught Ellen's hand. "They all like you," Skanasunk said. "They will not hurt you. You are my son." He drew himself up on his hams and announced: "We stay here."

6

The runners coming in during the third week in August reported the American army of six hundred men at Daudehokto, the village on the bend of the Alleghany only a few miles west. Before night half the village had packed up and taken the trail to Chenandoanes. The few who still remained stood silent, watching them go, the women toiling ahead up the steep trail, and the men a restless rear guard looking back. After they were gone the valley for a while seemed desolate. Night came with a scud of rain that dimmed the hilltops. The remaining men held another council. Seeing their relatives depart made them less certain of their own wisdom.

Newataquaah, alone in the house with Ellen, confided that it was Skanasunk's plan, if the others left, to take her and Ellen and Pete back into the hills and hide out until the army was out of the country. They would then return, using the caches of parched corn to live on, and building a new house.

But the army did not come. Next morning a solitary Indian with a bullet hole in his left arm came up the valley to inform them the army had headed back along its trail. They gave the Indian a feast.

After that life went on as it had before and the war no more affected them. The women followed their usual occupations and the men hunted. There were too few of them to drive deer, even with the children left, and they killed only half a dozen in four days. The wasp nests were built not very high that fall, and Skanasunk predicted a wet bad winter. The corn harvest at Tecarnohs was only fair.

The first snow came in November, a light, wet slush that set the small brooks flooding as it melted. Heavy mists hung in the valley, even during the days. The Indians seemed to feel it more than Ellen and Pete; they became silent, there was less laughter when the women visited.

It was during these weeks that Pete's uneasiness returned. He spent more time in the house, keeping Ellen company. His small black-Irish face sharpened. Once when they were alone he said, "I wish we'd gone back."

Ellen was surprised. "How could we have got back, Pete?"

"We could have taken Skanasunk's musket. The army wasn't more than a day's walk for us at Daudehokto."

"They wouldn't be going home."

"They'd have sent us back through Pennsylvania. Or we could've stayed. I like that westward country. We could've settled there."

"I like it better here."

He seemed to snap at her.

"How do you know? You've never seen it."

Ellen was placid. "Skanasunk and Newataquaah are staying here on account of us. We couldn't leave them if we wanted to. Not rightly, Pete."

"I guess that's so." Pete in his Indian dress looked small and unhappy. Ellen moved impulsively towards him, bent her face and kissed his lips.

She said, "I'll never marry anybody else but you, Pete."
Pete's face went white under the tan.

"You mean that?" he said huskily. And when she nodded,
"Honest to God? Cross your heart?" She nodded each
time. Her brown braids twitched beside the sharp little
points her breasts made under her overdress.

"Yes."

He tried to think of something more to say, and while
he fumbled in his mind, he heard Newataquaah returning.
Ellen heard her too. They moved apart from each other
and faced the door. Newataquaah was coughing. The
sound brought back to Pete the queer obsession of approaching death that had been troubling him.

Newataquaah was sick. As soon as she came through
the door both children realized that. She had been up
on the hillsides looking for dry wood. She was wet; and she
had a chill. As soon as she laid down her faggot, she
huddled beside the fire and asked Ellen to brew her some
hemlock tea.

Ellen boiled the hemlock tips in a small iron kettle and
dropped in maple sugar. Newataquaah always had a sweet
tooth. When the water had boiled, she lifted it off the
fire and handed it to Newataquaah who drank it from her
hominy ladle.

She said she felt better after she had drunk it all, and
smiled deprecatingly, as though she had made too much
fuss already. "We must cook the food for the men," she
said. But she did not look right to Ellen. There was a dark
flush in her cheeks and her eyes were too bright. When she
put her hand on the woman's forehead Ellen knew there

was fever. She said, "The men can wait. Now you are going to bed. You must take off those wet things and put on dry and I will heat your blankets." She hung a bearskin on the poles nearest the fire and several blankets, warming them thoroughly, while Newataquaah undressed in the cubicle. Before she had her dry clothes on, her teeth had begun to chatter again. But she would not lie down on the warm dry bed. She said, "All my life my man has come into his house and found me cooking food." But she seemed slow and Ellen did most of the work for her.

Newataquaah said several times, "I met Tekhatenhokwa's wife on the hill. She was really sick. I did not think she would get home. I had to carry down her wood."

"And then go back up for your own. I know," Ellen thought, reproaching herself that she had not gone also. One got so used to all the work Newataquaah did that one hardly noticed her. She was sitting down, swaying a little from the waist, forward over her knees. Ellen went quickly to her and pushed her back firmly onto the bearskin. "Peter! Peter!"

Peter, who had withdrawn while Newataquaah undressed, poked in his dark face.

"I think you'd better hunt up Skanasunk," Ellen said. "She's sick. I think she's very sick."

"What do you think she's got?"

"I don't know. I thought it was an ague; but it's some kind of a fever. Her breath sounds queer. I wish you'd go right off, Pete."

"All right," he said. "Don't get scared."

Newataquaah had begun to cough again. At times the

coughs seemed to choke her. Between coughs she kept shivering; but her forehead felt hot. Ellen brewed more tea. She had a vague idea that sweating would be good for a feverish person.

She thought that her mother would know what to do right away. But she didn't even know what was wrong. And lately she had been feeling like a grown-up woman. All at once it came to her that Newataquaah was really the only Indian in the village she knew well. It wasn't the Indian way of living that she liked; it was Newataquaah that made her think she liked it. She longed now for white towels to bathe the woman's face with, for a piece of camphor to keep the air pure, and above all for the conveniences of a good log cabin, with shelves and teakettles and spoons. Sitting on the edge of the cubicle she was aware of the Indian's brown hand reaching out to pat hers. "Don't look so afraid. I am a strong woman." The same sidelong smile in the brown face. "This is the first time I was ever sick, so I shall get well fast."

Peter came in with Skanasunk. The latter had been visiting in the village and smelled rank of tobacco. He stalked over and stood beside the cubicle with his arms folded.

"Are you sick?" he asked.

"I am sick." She said it apologetically, and added, "But not very sick."

"I think you are very sick," he replied, looking along his nose at her. "We have no healer now," he said sombrely. "She went away when the others did."

He ate a little from the stew Ellen had ready for him,

then got his blanket and hunched himself before the fire. He stayed that way all night. Ellen slept only in spells; whenever she looked up he was still there, looking down at the fire. But once he met her eyes and stared long at her. Then as the heavy coughing started again, he dropped his head.

In the morning, however, Newataquaah seemed a little brighter. She called Skanasunk and informed him she had dreamed of a falseface. It was not therefore a sickness but a demon in her. Skanasunk looked immeasurably relieved. He left the house at once, and as soon as he had gone, Newataquaah in a hoarse voice asked Ellen to prepare a feast for two people. "There are only two falsefaces in Tecarnohs now. They will come when it grows dark again."

Ellen had seen the falsefaces once visit a girl in the village who had sore eyes, and she was prepared for them. But it seemed fearful to have them come to one's own house. A little after dusk, she and Peter and Skanasunk heard the whisper of their shell rattles through the falling snow; and suddenly they were inside the door, two of them, in wooden masks with great stringy heads of false hair. The hideous faces were real enough in the firelight to have been alive, with the living eyes behind them; and yet they had no life.

They scuttered swiftly towards the fire, raising and lowering their faces with erratic jerks, while the bean seeds rattled softly in the turtle shells. They gathered ashes from the fire and approaching Newataquaah's cubicle powdered her with ashes. Then they made a circle of the fire, shaking their rattles here and there. Suddenly they joined and swooped upon Newataquaah. Ellen opened her mouth to protest as they seized the sick woman and three times forced her round the house between them.

She could not walk and her head wabbled on her shoulders. She tried feebly to follow their erratic steps. The sweat streamed down her face; her eyes were glazed and foolish; and when they finally flung her down on her blankets, her labored breathing sounded like the fading rattles. Before Ellen could cover her the falsefaces had gone.

Skanasunk sat with his head covered. Even Pete was wordless. It seemed crazy to Ellen. She did what she could to comb the mess of ashes out of Newataquaah's hair and wash her face. She did not dare undress her, overheated as she was, for the wind had come up and drafts were shaking the flames of the fire. But she reheated the food the falsefaces had not tasted and they ate together, without speaking. When she went out into the little vestibule for more wood she saw that it was snowing heavily.

Newataquaah seemed no better in the morning. After eating, Skanasunk left the house. He was gone all morning. The snow stopped towards noon and a high wind cut through the valley from the north, clearing the pine boughs of white, and humming through the hardwood limbs. Peter hung round the house. He did not speak much except to whisper, "Do you think she's going to die?" Ellen did not know what to answer. She only knew that Newataquaah was desperately sick. Towards dark Skanasunk returned from a second expedition. He had a snowbird in a little basket. This he hung at the far end of the house; and after it had been there a little while the bird began to make small twittering notes.

It twittered during the night from time to time. Ellen heard it over the wind. She would have liked to set it free; but Pete told her not to touch it. "I don't know what he wants it for; but I followed him this afternoon. He's been digging a hole."

"He thinks she's going to die!"

"I guess he does. Tekhatenhokwa's squaw died yesterday and there's a lot more sick. Half the Indians is sick with the same disease, I guess." Pete shivered. After black dark, Ellen felt shivery too. In lulls of the wind she could hear shrill screaming wails of Indian women in the village. Even the bird hushed when they were audible.

Skanasunk sat beside Newataquaah's cubicle. The white children sat together. "If it wasn't bad weather, I'd leave here," Pete whispered.

He started suddenly. Ellen got to her feet, walked round Skanasunk, and looked into the cubicle. She didn't feel sure. But Skanasunk said, "She is dead." He had not moved.

Ellen gave way to an inexplicable burst of rage. She pointed a finger at Skanasunk and cried out, "You knew she was dying. You didn't say anything. You didn't even move when she died!" She burst into a storm of tears. She had a glimpse of Peter's face turned suddenly white and sharp. But she could not stand it. She flung herself into her own cubicle and covered herself with her robes, trying to shut out the Indian house. But it could not be shut out.

The smell of the skins covering her was Indian. The smoke was Indian. It was not clean. It was terrifying.

Peter sneaked up to her and touched the mound of blankets.

"Ellen," he whispered.

Her muffled voice answered him: "Leave me alone!"

But he kept his hand on the blankets. She could feel the pressure of it as though he were afraid to let go of her. Even though she cried, "Go away," she was glad that he kept his hand there.

7

Skanasunk took no notice of her or of Pete. He continued to sit by the fire, unmoving, his big-nosed face like a carved image. In the morning Pete went to the village and gave the news of Newataquaah's death and a few Indians came up to the house to condole with the relatives. The women got Ellen aside to weep with them, but she did not want to weep. Newataquaah dead was not the same to her. She was not a human being any more. She was a dead Indian. The women glanced askance at Ellen for making so little noise. They finally asked her when she was going to dress the body so it could be buried: but Ellen could not bear to touch it.

The women did the work and left without addressing her. When they had gone Skanasunk rose and ordered Ellen to bring a kettle of food uncooked, some burning punk, and a little faggot of sticks. He told Peter to carry the bird in the little basket. Then he himself picked up Newataquaah and carried her from the house.

There was no fog that day; a new snow had begun to fall, a cold driving storm of dry hard flakes. Even in the thick grove of hemlocks where the Indian finally stopped, it sifted down with a continual sibilance through the heavy branches.

There was a round hole in the snow, in which Skanasunk placed the body, crouching slightly, the sightless eyes turned eastward. Beside the body he placed the filled kettle. Then he covered the hole with limb wood and piled earth in a mound upon it. He stood still a while when he was done before he took the basket from Pete and opened the cover.

The little snowbird hopped up on the rim, clasping it with his wiry toes. Suddenly, with a soft twitter it let go and flipped up into the branches. None of them could follow it far in the snow. As soon as it had disappeared, Skanasunk knelt down and started a small fire. They left while it still crackled brightly, a tiny spot of color in the black and white of woods and snow.

8

Skanasunk had changed. The whole village had changed. As the snow drifted in it seemed like death made visible. Three of Tekhatenhokwa's children died after the coming of the new year. He died himself two weeks later and there was no relative to bury or make a lamentation. The snow had become so deep and the ground so frozen that the bodies could not be buried but were left on tree platforms in the ancient fashion. The Indians seemed to have no resistance to the disease, but neither Pete nor Ellen caught it. Once an Indian woman stopped Ellen and said, "The Honundeonts have said we were not sick this way before white people came." Ellen did not know what to answer and hurried home; but she could feel the woman's eyes following her and hear her heavy coughing. None of the Indians laughed any more. She remembered how Newataquaah, and even Skanasunk, used to laugh. He had changed more than the others. He would sit by the fire hour after hour following Ellen's motions with his black eyes. He made her nervous and afraid. She asked Pete to stay near by, one day.

"Why?" asked Pete.

"I don't know. He makes me afraid. He does not speak." She shivered a little. "I know he's thinking about me. But I don't know what."

Pete, studying her, suddenly thought he understood. Ellen was growing up faster than he was. But he didn't say so to her. He merely made a point of never going out of call while Skanasunk was in the house. At night, the two of them sat together on the other side of the fire, whispering to each other if they had anything to say. "Do Indians go crazy?" Ellen asked.

"Everything goes crazy," Pete said. "Even hedgehogs do, I guess."

Ellen had to work hard, doing all the work for herself

and two men. It left her tired-out at night, and easy to frighten. She shuddered when Pete said that.

"We'll leave here when the snow goes," Pete said. He began turning over plans in his mind.

That night Skanasunk began to cough. He lay in his cubicle for days, or dragged himself out to the fire like a dog and sat huddled close up to it. He hardly ate at all; and the flesh seemed to shrink on his skull, so that his eyes appeared to hang loose in overlarge sockets. It required all the fortitude she could muster for Ellen to nurse him the three days he was sickest, and she had to get Peter to help move him. Skanasunk dreamed of a falseface as Newataquaah had done, but Ellen would not let Pete find the surviving one to come and dance. She thought now that it was the falsefaces as much as the disease that had killed Newataquaah. She did not know why she worked so hard to save the Indian, but at times she felt that Newataquaah was near by watching, and she was afraid not to help him. She had a presentiment of Newataquaah's presence whenever she saw a snowbird. There was one especially that seemed to hang round the house with no logical persistence. Sometimes she felt that Pete hoped Skanasunk might die; but she would not let herself give way. Her thin face acquired a new determination.

Skanasunk survived. The sickness left him so weak, however, that Peter felt he could leave the house safely and went out hunting for fresh meat, staying away all day. During that day, when Ellen gave him his food, Skanasunk broke his long silence.

"Listen to me."

She looked up from her own ladle.

"Yes, Hanih." She gave him the Indian name for "father."

"Listen to me," he repeated. She had a strange feeling that the intentness in his black eyes had taken her own and fixed them, so that she could not turn her own away. "Newataquaah is dead. Skanasunk has no wife. Skanasunk has no mother. You have no mother. So Skanasunk must speak himself." He drew his breath so lightly his chest hardly rose. "Skanasunk is not your Hanih. You are white."

As he paused she at last managed to wrench her eyes away.

"Listen to me. A young girl should marry an old man. It is the ancient law. It is better that way. Skanasunk is not old but he is a good man. *Hano!*"

Ellen had no idea what she should do or say. She could only cry, "Peter, Peter," silently. She could not answer Skanasunk. She could only stare at his sunken face which seemed to her to have become cruel and ruthless, as cold and flat-cheeked as an eagle's. When after a while he said, "I am still sick," she could stand it no longer.

She was like a little girl running out of the house. She caught up her faggot strap from the vestibule as an excuse, and all that afternoon she dawdled on the hillside watching for Pete's return.

She intercepted him on the hill trail and blurted out her news before he could begin speaking. He had half a doe, cut up, and he listened to her with his face intent and white.

"We can't go now," he said. "The snow's plain slush.

It'll be two weeks before we can travel, even if the weather holds warm."

"I want to go now. I can keep up with you. The snow's not so deep."

Pete with his long mussed hair looked wild and frightened.

"Stop blatting, can't you? We've got to wait till the snow's gone. Anybody could track us now." He stopped, looking down at the musket. "We've got to wait till we can travel fast. There's only powder for about four shots left. We can't use it hunting." •

She hadn't thought of that. Nobody had been out of Tecarnohs to trade since the middle of last summer. "Can't you shoot a bow and arrow?"

"No," he said glumly. "Only Indians are good at that." Then he became practical again. "I've got the other half of this doe hung up. I'll smoke it tomorrow. Maybe in ten days we can start."

9

The weather held. The late March thawing took the snow from the woods but left the brooks so high they made hard crossing. Ellen and Pete had crossed the Genesee on a raft, headed north of the Conhocton, and made the southern circuit of the lakes. At the head of both Seneca and Cayuga they found marks of the Continental Army and rummaged twice in burnt towns, looking for corn.

The trip had taken longer than they had expected. Their

venison had given out and their corn was low. But the Indian towns offered nothing but charred logs of the houses. No trees were left standing. They were desolate, untracked except by porcupines and mice. Ellen found a powder-horn dropped by a soldier, but it was empty.

At night Peter cut hemlock boughs with Skanasunk's war hatchet and they slept close together, doubling their blankets. They had encountered the tracks of about forty men, mostly Indians, on the Conhocton, and considering it a war party Peter had doubled west and north to find a swamp where they could lose their own trail, spending two days in the process.

Ellen followed him blindly, accepting his lead. She felt completely secure in his knowledge of the woods, know-ing that as long as she could follow him far enough, he would lead her into the Mohawk Valley. The trouble was to keep walking. They did not talk much, even at night, when they lay together in their flimsy lean-tos. They were too exhausted and too cold; for, after seeing the track of the war party, Pete refused to build fires.

It was the day after they had crossed the headwaters of the Owego River that they began to feel that they were being followed. By then they were so short of food that the few grains of parched corn Pete doled out were not enough to warm them. A heavy frost had settled, and finally Pete agreed they must have a fire.

They built a small one and huddled over it, luxuriating in the strange sensation of outer warmth. Looking across it at Ellen, Pete was struck by her thinness. She had never been a stout girl; but now the skin looked frail on her cheeks, almost papery. He felt that if he threw a grain of gravel at her it would pass through.

Her face looked immeasurably older and grey under the weather burn. It made her brown hair seem darker colored and more heavy. He said suddenly, "You're a pretty good girl, Ellen. You ain't made a fuss at all, even when I got twisted sometimes." She only smiled a little. Her back was slumped and she hugged her knees, resting her chin on them. Her knees had grown knobby as she lost flesh.

Finally she asked, "How much farther is it, do you think?"

"I don't know. I guess it's a week's travel to the Unadilla maybe."

"Then how far?"

"Two days into German Flats for us."

"Nine days isn't so long a time."

He said abruptly, "If I see a deer tomorrow I'll take a chance and shoot it."

She started to smile, started to say, "That's wonderful," but suddenly her lips grew wet; and then she buried her face and started crying. It was while she was crying that Pete saw the snowbird and said, "That's queer."

"What is?"

"That snowbird. It's about dark. I've hardly ever seen one so late in spring either."

She stopped crying to look at the little bird. The sight of it made her remember Newataquaah, and so she thought of Skanasunk. They had slipped out one morning, Pete first, to collect the jerked deer meat; she later, pretending

to go for wood, and meeting him on the hill over the
village. They had gone down the far side, climbing over
rocky places to hide their trail and then wading a small
brook for nearly a mile. By dusk, Pete figured they had
had a seven-mile start.

They watched the snowbird hang around for several
minutes, and after it was gone crept under their hemlock
lean-to. They could still feel the fire's warmth against their
feet. But Ellen woke Pete several times by talking in her
sleep about Newataquaah and Skanasunk. She made him
uneasy. In the morning he did what he had not done for
several days. He scouted round the camp.

He found no tracks that looked human. But he did find
a black squirrel dead under a tree and there was nothing to
show how it had died. When he picked it up he saw its
neck was broken; but he had never heard of a squirrel
dying of a broken neck. He carried it back to their camp
and they roasted it over a small fire. He told Ellen, however, that he had decided not to shoot that day as long as
they had been so lucky as to find the squirrel.

A little after noon, though, he came on the track of a
single Indian and the track was fresh. Ellen saw it too.
It was following a small deer run eastward. Both of them
realized then how fortunate it was they had not tried to
hunt a deer.

Pete thought they ought to follow the trail to see where
the man was heading. They went very slowly, making no
sound, until finally it brought them to a camp site where
half a dozen Indians had spent the night.

Pete made Ellen stand still off the run while he rummaged round the tracks. When he returned to her, his face was troubled. "Our man joined up with the others. They broke camp, but he turned back, so he's somewhere back of us now."

10

The next two days they hurried. But they saw nothing. They began to get desperate for food, so that Ellen kept eyeing even the robins hungrily. Pete looked for hedge-hogs, hoping to find one on the ground. But all the hedge-hogs they saw were well up in trees and seemed inclined to stay there. Then, on the third day, as they followed another deer path, they found one lying dead.

They stopped where they were and made a fire and feasted, too hungry even to question their providence until they had done eating. Peter, finally brought to a sense of his own carelessness, dragged Ellen off the path and made her hide under a stony hill while he scouted. Again he found the tracks of one man. They led him due north and then east for nearly a mile and were lost in a shallow river crossing.

Pete studied the river thoughtfully. The trunk of an enormous hemlock lay out into the ford under the water and two huge roots, upended, were joined like praying hands. The queerness of the tree raised an echo of something he had been told. Suddenly he remembered. Honus had said it was the best lower crossing of the Unadilla.

He lay on the bank for a long time, staring across the

smooth slide of brown water without seeing anything. After sunset he went back for Ellen and told her they had reached the Unadilla. He led her in a wide sweep northward, telling her they would follow to the mouth of Butternut Creek, head through the Edmeston Patent and go overland west of Andrustown. He knew that way, once he had found Butternut Creek.

Now they could travel at night, having a moon. They made fair progress, spotted the Butternut in the grey dawn. They were going to cross when an owl began hooting from the far bank.

Pete stood stock-still.

"Listen," he whispered. "That ain't no bird."

Ellen could not tell.

"Listen how it goes."

"I don't know."

"We better wait. It don't sound right to me."

As they waited, a line of men bunched on the bank above them. Then they lined out again over the river. Their shapes were dark shadows against the water, holding guns above their heads. But even in the darkness the children could make out that the arms were bare.

"Indians," Pete breathed into her ear. After an hour of silence they heard an owl hoot again. He said, "That's a natural sounding owl." It came from the far side of the river. "We'll chance crossing."

11

It was next morning on the hills south of German Flats that they were sure. Pete had said, "That sounds like a deer ahead." But they did not care. They were only two hours from the forts. They could already see the wide expanse of sky that meant the valley between the trunks of the trees ahead.

It was a day of bright sunlight. The naked brow of the hill with the dead winter's grass dry underfoot gave them a view of the forts on each side of the river, the burned sites of settlers' houses, and men plowing the ground while a guard surrounded the field they worked in.

Then, as they stepped over the edge of the hill, they saw a feathered arrow stuck in the ground. Beside it was a blue square of calico and on the calico were laid two fox's ears, and a little silver brooch of Indian make.

"It's Newataquaah's," Ellen exclaimed. "What are the fox ears for?"

"It's Skanasunk. So we would know who the brooch was from if you didn't recognize it."

"You mean he left it for us?"

"I guess. I guess it was him, all along."

Pete was lost in thought. Then he set the musket down, the musket he had never fired on all their long journey, with the powderhorn beside it. "He's hanging round somewhere. He'll find it all right. But I guess he means for me to take the arrow. I guess he didn't have nothing else for me."

12

Long after the war, when she had been Mrs. Peter Kelly for many years, Ellen used to like to wear the brooch. The children often humored her by asking why she wore a queer thing like it, and then she would tell them about how she and Mr. Kelly lived among the Indians.

DYGARTSBUSH

JOHN BORST was the first settler to return to Dygartsbush after the war. He came alone in the early fall of 1784, on foot, carrying a rifle, an axe, a brush scythe, a pair of blankets, and a sack of cornmeal. He found the different lots hard to recognize, for there was no sign left of the houses. Only the charred butt logs remained, surrounding a layer of dead coals that the rain had long since beaten into the earth. The fields had gone to brush; the piece where he had had his corn was covered with a scrub of berry vines, rough grass, yarrow, and steeplebush. Young poplars had begun to come in along the edge. But near the center of it he found a stunted, slender little group of tiny cornstalks, tasseled out, with ears that looked like buds.

Whenever the work of clearing brush seemed everlasting he would go over and look at that corn and think how good his first crop seven years ago had looked. It was good land, with a southerly slope and water near by. That was why he had come back to it. Other people were pushing westward; many of them Yankees from New England who had seen something of the country during the war or heard tell of it from returning soldiers. But John Borst thought it would be many years after their farms became productive before they would find a market for their crops. The war had taught him to prefer the things he knew and remembered.

After he found that his wife had been taken captive to

the Indians' towns, he had joined the army. They had given him a fifty-dollar bounty and a uniform. As soon as his enlistment ended he volunteered from his militia class for the levies and was assigned the land bounty of two hundred acres. This he had left with Mr. Paris of Stone Arabia, who was now with the Legislature in New York City, to sell for him on a commission basis.

If he were lucky enough to sell, he would become comparatively rich; but John Borst was a methodical man who did not believe in waiting for good luck. When he had his land readied again and his house rebuilt it would be time enough to think of buying stock and household goods.

He needed next to nothing now. He lived on his cornmeal and pigeons he knocked off a roosting tree at dusk each evening. All his daylight hours he spent in the field, cutting down the brush and arranging it for burning. He slept in a small lean-to he had set up the first day. And it was at night as he lay in his blankets and watched the fire dying that he felt lonely. He had had no inclination to remarry, though he knew of several men whose women had been carried off by the Indians who had taken new wives in the past year. One of the Devendorf girls in Fort Plain he thought would marry him if he asked her. She had been pretty open about it, too. She wasn't a bad girl either and he had thought seriously whether he would not be wise to take her. But that would have meant building a cabin first off for her to live in; and now that he was back on the land he knew he would have begrudged the time spent raising one and the money necessary to hire help, since there were no neighbors to come to a raising bee. Besides he had never got over his feeling that Delia would come back. He felt it more strongly here in Dygartsbush than he had in the past seven years.

At night he would remember her in their one month of married life — cooking his supper for him when he came in; the way she knelt in front of the fire and handled the pans and dishes; sitting beside him fixing his clothes after the meal; getting ready for bed when he had stepped outside the last thing: he would come in to find her in her nightdress, combing her brown hair before the hearth, and the light of the red coals showed him the shadow of her body. She had been a long-bodied girl with fine square shoulders; she stood straight, even after a day of helping him in the corn piece; at night, when she must have felt tired, she seemed able to renew her vigor and his with it. He did not think that the Devendorf girl would work the way Delia had and seem happy and gay in the labor.

He worked alone all through September. In October, when the dry winds began to parch the ground, he burned his land. Then, when he was ready to return to Fort Plain, three men turned up in Dygartsbush.

When he first sighted them, he went over to the edge of the burning for his rifle. There had been cases during the past two years of settlers who had gone back to their farms being murdered by Indians or renegades. But the men shouted to him that they were friends and as they came nearer he saw that one of them was Honus Kelly.

With Kelly were two New Englanders named Hartley and Phelps who came to look over the land. Honus explained that he had decided to sell his lot and that he had the selling of the Dygarts' also. As both these touched on John Borst's land, John spent a day with them running the boundaries. Hartley and Phelps liked the country and suggested to John that the four of them raise three cabins so that they could move into them in the spring.

John had not figured on building his cabin that fall; but the men had horses to skid the logs and it seemed like a good chance to get his house built without using cash. He spent half that night deciding that he would build his new house exactly on the site of the old one. When Honus Kelly asked him why, he replied that in 1776 it had seemed to him the best site and he had found no reason to change his mind now. Kelly laughed and said it was just Dutch stubbornness and Hartley said he thought it would make uneasy living, there might be ghosts around. "Nobody got killed here," John explained. In the back of his mind, however, was the thought of how it would seem to Delia when she came back. With the cabin raised the place would look to her the way it had the day he had brought her in the first time. "My, it's a nice house, it's a nice place, John. I think it's beautiful." He remembered her words, her fresh deep voice, and the sudden springing of her breasts under her laced bodice. That was the first time she had not sounded shy. All the way in she had been shy with him, so that he had wondered whether he had been too strong with her. He was a big, powerful, heavy man, and like most slow-moving men he did not realize his full strength.

They built the three cabins in the next three weeks, cutting and skidding the logs with the New Englanders' horses; and then John helped them burn their land with the brush standing; and then they left to file their deeds and return to New England for their families. They would come back, they said, as soon as the roads were passable.

"Ain't you coming out with us, John?" Honus asked him.

John said no. He would stay and do finishing work on his cabin and maybe fell some timber over in the hardwood lot. He would want to put in wheat next fall. The price of wheat was bound to go up with the influx of new settlers.

Honus did not laugh at him. "You're right," he said. Then he added, "They're going to have a treaty with the Indians this month. They're going to ask for all prisoners to get sent back."

"That's good," John said. He stood stubbing his toes in the dirt as if to settle his feet.

"Delia ought to be back next summer," Honus said understandingly. "They wouldn't kill a girl like her. They liked her." He turned to the two New Englanders. "I'd probably have my hair hanging on an Indian post right now if it wasn't for John's wife. She helped me get away after they took us. They killed every other man but me and my brother and John here. Delia's a fine girl; she'll make a good neighbor for your families."

John flushed. Phelps, the older of the two, said it would be fine for his wife to have a woman neighbor. Especially for his mother-in-law who didn't like the idea of their coming. He would tell his mother-in-law about Mrs. Borst.

"Tell her she's pretty," said Honus. "One of the prettiest women I ever saw."

John did not flush again. It was a fact, not flattery. The younger man, Hartley, looked round the clearing as if he were trying to imagine what an Indian raid was like. "Must've been pretty bad," he said.

Honus said, "It was bad enough." And they left.

It seemed lonelier to John the day after they left. He had got to like them. They didn't seem like Yankees, especially. It would be good to have neighbors, he thought. Delia would like it. She used to say she liked people round, not that she liked to gad a lot, but just to hear and see them every week or so."

The rainy weather set in and he hunted him a deer and then spent time in his new cabin chinking the walls. The men had had some paper which he used in his window and the inside of the cabin he fixed up with shelves like the old one; but these were made of split logs, like the benches. He would have to buy boards for a table, or buy a table second hand.

He went out when the snow came, and worked at what he could find around Fort Plain and then trapped a little. In the spring he had thirty dollars left of his bounty money and thirty-five dollars from trapping over and above the cost of the traps. He bought a mare for thirty-five dollars, a heifer in calf for twelve, and three hogs for four dollars at a bargain. With what was left he bought his corn seed, a log chain and a plough, and hired a man to help him drive in his stock.

It was a bare beginning; but he considered himself well

off. He was starting his planting when the Phelpses came in: Phelps, his wife, one child, and Mrs. Cutts, his mother-in-law, a thin-faced woman with a dry way of speaking. John Borst got to like her pretty well.

The Hartleys came later, hardly in time to plant, and John Borst thought he would not make as good a neighbor. He said he was late because he did not like slush traveling; he wanted to have warm weather to settle. He got John and Phelps to lend him a hand with his first field.

Mrs. Hartley was a frightened acting girl who seemed to take a fancy to John. She was always running over to the Borst place to be neighborly, offering to mend his things. Once she took some home with her when she found he was out. He went over next day to get them back and thank her, and looking round her cabin he thought privately that if Mrs. Hartley put her mind to it she would find so much trouble catching up on her own work that she would not have time to take on his. She made him take back a loaf of bread, and when he got home he found that it was soggy in the middle.

But he had to admit that the sight of even Mrs. Hartley, who was a pretty-looking girl for all her sloppy ways, made him lonely. Next day, though he could have put off the trip for another week, he went out to Fort Plain for flour and stopped in to see Honus Kelly. He asked Honus whether any women had been brought in from the Indian towns.

Honus thought quite a few had. "They most of them get left at Fort Stanwix." He seemed to understand how John felt. "Anyway, when Delia shows up she'll most probably come through here. I'll tell her you're back at Dygartsbush."

"Thanks," said John. He fumbled round for a minute. "Do you think there's any chance of her coming back?"

"Sure I do. I told you before the Indian that took her treated her real good. Pete told you that, too." Honus didn't feel it was his business to tell John the old Indian planned to make a squaw of her.

"Yes, you told me that." John Borst looked out the window. "I wonder if it would do any good if I went out looking for her. They say it's safe enough traveling in the Indian country."

"You'd probably never find her that way. She might turn up just after you left here and then you both would have that much more time waiting."

"I guess that's right." Honus had told him that before, too. Honus knew a lot about the Indian country. A man wouldn't have any chance out there finding out about a particular white woman. He said good-bye to Honus and went over to the store to do his trading. He bought himself some flour and a bag of salt and some salt beef. He didn't know quite how it was but when he happened to see a new bolt of dress goods he decided to buy some. Later he decided it was because the brown striping reminded him of the color of her hair. He told the storekeeper's wife he wanted enough for a tall girl, about so high, and he held his hand level with his cheekbones.

He started back about two hours before sunset, though he knew that he would have to go slow the last part of

the way as the mare was still unfamiliar with the trail. It
was after dark when he reached the outskirts of Dygartsbush, and he could see off on his left the light from the
Hartleys' cabin, a single small square glow appearing and
disappearing among the trees with the mare's progress. He
had a glimpse of Mrs. Hartley crossing the lighted space.
She had her hair down her back, as though she were
preparing for the night. The sight brought him a sense of
intimacy from which he himself was excluded. He had
no companionship but the sound of the mare's hoofs, the
smell of sweat, and the motion of her walk between his
legs.

He did not see any light from Phelps's, but he heard
the child crying. The thin sound was muffled. John knew
that the child and the grandmother slept in the loft. By
the time he reached his own clearing the sound of crying
had died away and he was alone with the mare under a
dark sky. He rode heavily, leaning his hands on her
withers, paying no attention to the trail; and he was entirely unprepared when the mare threw up her head and
stopped short, snorting.

She nearly unseated him and as it was his cheek struck
painfully against her head. He started to kick her sides,
jerking her head angrily, when she moved forward again
of her own accord but with her head still raised and ears
pointed. Looking up himself, he saw at the far end of
the clearing a light in his own window.

It made a dim orange pattern through the paper panes.
He could see no shadow of any person moving in the
house but a spark jumping from the chimney mouth

caught his eye and he guessed someone had freshened a fire on the hearth.

He stopped the mare and dismounted and got his rifle ready in his hand. Honus had told him that there were still a few Tories and Indians who had lived along the valley who were trying to get back. Down in Fort Plain they had an organization to deal with them.

He knew how far the light reached when the door was opened. Before he came into the area he let the mare have her head and slapped her flank. She stepped ahead quickly, passing the door to go round to the shed. John lay down in the grass with his rifle pointed.

The door opened, shedding its light over the mare; but there was no ambush from the field. A whippoorwill had started singing but John did not hear it. A woman was standing in the door looking out with large eyes at the mare. The beast stopped again, snorting uneasily, then moved on. The woman cupped her hands on each side of her face to act as blinders from the light and stepped past the mare. He could see her plain now. She wore Indian clothes, moccasins and skirt and a loose overdress. He could tell by her height who she was.

He got up slowly, a little uncertain in his arms and legs, walked over to her, and leaned on his rifle and looked into her face to make sure.

But he knew anyway. She stood erect, looking back at him, her hands hanging at her sides. He did not think she had changed, except for her Indian clothes and the way she wore her hair in two braids over her breast. He saw her lips part to say, "I'm back, John," but her voice was the barest whisper. He shifted a little so that her face, turning with him, came into the light, showing him again after seven years the curve of her cheek and the tenderness of her mouth. Then he saw that her eyes were wet. Neither of them heard the whippoorwill still calling in the young corn.

2

At times, John Borst had the feeling that he and Delia had taken up their lives exactly where they were the night the Indians raided Dygartsbush. That night also he had been coming home from Fort Plain with flour, almost at the same time. But then he had been afoot instead of riding his own mare.

That night might have been a dream—the burning cabins and the firing, and the rain. He had come into Hawyer's clearing just in time to see the Indians reach that place. He could tell by the fires that the Indians had surrounded every house. He had seen Hawyer shot in his door and Mrs. Hawyer hauled out of the house. The Indian had her by the hair and was dragging her the way a man might lug along a stubborn dog to put it out for the night. Then they had spotted John, half a dozen of them, and he had set out to run for the Fort.

He told Delia about it the day after her return (they had not done any talking that first night). He told her how he had got fifteen men to come back with him and they had found every house in ashes. They had picked up the tracks at the end of his lot, followed them for half a dozen miles. Then they had come back and buried the dead. That task had taken them the rest of the day. They had had to camp the night just off Hawyer's clearing and it was sheer luck that John had waked to hear the crying of a little girl. He said if he had not heard it then Mrs. Dygart's daughters would probably have wandered off and got lost in the woods. When he found them they were walking away from the ashes of the Dygart house because the seven-year-old one did not think it was theirs. She was hauling the little one along trying to find their house. When they heard him coming they just crouched down, still as rabbits. Now, he said, they were with their mother, who had been brought back by General Sullivan's army.

He watched Delia. She had been crouching in front of the fire, like an Indian squaw, and while he talked she had suddenly got down on her knees, the way she used to do. It gave him a vaguely uneasy feeling to see the slow pink rising in her cheeks, as though she had corrected herself in a mistake. Now she lifted her face and her eyes regarded him with their old searching level glance.

"Did you think I was dead, John?"

He thought a while. "No. I didn't think so. But I thought I probably wouldn't ever see you again. I joined the army. There wasn't anything left for me here, and I didn't get back to Tryon County for more'n a year. Then I found out that Caty Breen had got back. She came back married to a man that had got himself exchanged. I don't remember his name. She's living up in Kingsland now."

Delia said, "I'm glad. She was so scared. They took her off from the rest of us, two Indians did." She turned her attention back to her cooking.

"Where was that?" he asked.

"Near the head of a river. I don't know what one. We went on to the Genesee, the rest of us, except for Peter Kelly and the Mitchel girl."

"They got back four years ago," John told her. "They ran away. Honus told me about it. He told me Pete hadn't heard anything of you."

"Honus was good to me, John."

"He told me how you helped him get away."

"What else did he tell you?"

John looked at her. "Why, I don't know. Just about how he got away. He kept telling me, too, he didn't think the Indians would hurt you any. He said the one that took you thought a lot of you. He had a comic name — High-Grass, I think Honus said."

"Yes, High-Grass. Gasotena."

She drew her breath slowly, and became quite still. He had noticed that about her in the one day she had been home — the way she fell into a stillness. Not silence, for she always answered him at once if he said anything. He did not know how to describe it to himself, but he supposed it was because she felt some kind of strangeness getting back to white people. Maybe, he thought, she felt strange with him. Seven years was a long time to be away from a man; maybe a woman got to feeling different about things.

He said, "It must be queer, coming back to me after so

long. Must seem like taking up with a man without getting married, almost." He tried to say it in a light, joking kind of way.

But she whirled suddenly, lifting her face and looking closely into his. "What makes you say that?" He saw her lips tremble and become still.

"I didn't mean to make you jump. I thought, maybe, I'd seem like almost a strange man. Like, maybe, there was things you'd disremembered about me. Things, maybe, you didn't like so well."

He could see her throat fill and empty.

"Did you think that last night?"

He felt himself coloring. "No."

"Are there things about me?"

"No," he said. "God, no." There was visible pain in her eyes. He was a fool, he thought. "Look out, Delia. That fat's catching fire."

She turned back to the cooking quickly and silently, and he looked down on her back. It always seemed to him the most homely thing in the world for a man to sit watching his wife bend to cook his dinner. She had done up her hair in braids wound round her head, but she still wore her Indian clothing. It was good to work in, she said. They couldn't afford to throw away good clothes. Now she was still again for a long time, and he thought she had gone off into one of her spells until she began to speak.

Then her voice was throaty and pitched low and she seemed to have difficulty with her words. It was hard to hear her. One of the hogs had wandered up to the shed door and was oinking to himself and rubbing his hide against the doorjamb. Her words came through the sound of the pig and the dead June heat.

She said: "I used to wonder if you'd got caught. But they never brought in your scalp. I got to believe you were alive, John. Then after I'd been in the Indian town for a while I began to think I'd have to stay there all my life. We knew the army was coming. I thought it might come near; but it never did come near. Then after a long time it seemed as if I didn't have anything to hope for. I wasn't bad off like some other prisoners. The Indians were good to me. But it wasn't like white people being good to you. I didn't mind the work, John. Work helped, somehow. But no work you did was for yourself. No house belongs to any one person among the Indians. Their gardens are for the whole house, all the people in it. The squaws didn't ever plant flowers by their houses. I used to think about the little dark red pinks I planted just outside the door and wonder if they ever blowed."

Listening to her in a kind of fascination John heard himself say, "I don't know, Delia," but she went on quietly: —

"I guess the fire scorched them to death. I looked for them when I came back but it was getting near dark then so I couldn't tell. I looked this morning, but there weren't any. Indians don't plant flowers, though they like picking wild ones. The children would pick wild ones and carry them round till they were dead and throw them away. I put some in water once to show them but they never caught on. Sometimes I used to think maybe you had come back and was tending the pinks for me. But I knew that was silly, that you couldn't come back till the war was over."

She drew a long breath.

"I used to wonder and wonder about you, what you were doing, and who you were with, John. Did you wonder about me?"

"Yes."

"When they told me about the treaty and said I could go home, I was afraid, John. I thought, it's seven years and you haven't heard from me. I thought maybe you'd found another woman and married her."

"I saw plenty," he said. "I never had the urge to marry."

"I didn't know that. I wouldn't have blamed you, though. But I had to come back to find out. Ganowauges brought me. He knew the southern way better and he said he'd bring me as far as Fort Plain. Most went to Fort Stanwix, I think. I asked him if we could come through here and he said we could do it. We got here just about dark, John. We came in the same way Gasotena took me away. We came out of the woods and we both smelled hoed land. Then I looked and saw the house — just the way it was, right in the same place. I was so frightened I could scarcely move. Ganowauges pointed to it and told me to go. I asked him if he would wait. I thought then I would go back with him if there was a woman in it. He acted kind of nervy and said he'd rather wait in the woods. I went to the house, John. I had to see what she looked like."

"She wasn't there, was she?"

Delia glanced at him in a startled way, saw his eyes, and tried to smile.

"No. First I thought maybe you'd taken her to Fort Plain with you. Then I went inside and I saw you'd been living alone."

"How did you know that?"

She smiled this time, to herself.

"I knew it was you, too. I could tell because the way the tooth twig was laid against the sack of gunpowder. You always laid it standing up so the brush end would dry out. It was so much the same. I just sat down and cried. I didn't want to light the light because I wanted to get my crying done before you came. I forgot all about Ganowauges. I never even thanked him. John, did you build the house right here on purpose?"

He said, "Yes."

He saw her eyelids trembling and got up and went out to wash. When he came in again she seemed peaceful. She had laid out their food on the board table. He said, "It's not so well fixed. But I'll get a glass sash before winter and a chest of drawers for you to keep your clothes in. I've got a little money left."

She drew a deep breath, looking round. "It's all ours. John, I don't care if we're poor. It's no matter to me. All I want to do is work for you and for you to be happy, and have you care for me the way you used to. I'm older than I was. I guess I show it. But I'm healthy and strong, still."

Her voice tailed off. He said, "You look all right."

He felt strangely troubled. He could not tell why. He tried to talk about something else. "I'll have to take you over to the neighbors. They're Yankee people. But I like the Phelpses. I like Mrs. Cutts, too. She's kind of like the way Mrs. Staats was, but she's sensible."

"Which one is she?"

"Mrs. Phelps's mother. She's elderly. Hartleys are always borrowing. You'll have to watch out for them. They mean all right. They're just shiftless." He got up. "Guess I'll begin mowing grass over in the swale this afternoon. We got to have hay for the mare and cow, next winter."

"We didn't have a cow and horse before, did we? It makes it seem more like a farm even if we haven't got a glass window. When's the cow due?"

"They thought in September. I think maybe August. I had a chance to get her cheap," he explained. "I meant to get a window first."

"I'd rather have the cow. I used to make butter fine."

John went out, leaving her looking happy, he thought. More the way she used to be. He took his scythe and went towards the swale; but as soon as he entered the woods he made a circuit and picked up Delia's tracks. He found the Indian's plain enough. The Indian had been like a fox nosing the clearing. After Delia went towards the house, he had moved along the edge of the woods until he was opposite the door. There in crushed ferns John found the imprint of the Indian's body. He must have lain there for quite a while. Probably he had been there when John came home. John stood still thinking what a plain mark he must have made. He didn't like the thought of it even though the Indian hadn't done anything.

Delia came to the door with the bucket she had been

washing the dishes in and threw away the water with a swinging motion, making a sparkle of drops through the sunlight. Then she stood for a moment resting her weight on one hip and staring after the way John had gone. He thought he had never seen her look so pretty as she did in her Indian dress. Just why he wasn't sure. He thought maybe it was the strangeness of it — as if she were something he didn't really have a right to. After a moment, she let her head bend, and then she turned and put up her arm against the jamb of the door and rested her forehead on it. She might have been crying.

Suddenly it came to John that he was spying on his wife. His face reddened, even though he knew himself alone and unobserved; and he went back through the edge of the woods, cut across to the swale, and set down the point of the scythe snathe in the grass.

He began whetting the scythe. The high sound of the stone against the blade, the heat of the sun on the back of his neck, the waves of warm air shimmering above the grass, and the whine of a hot-weather bird all seemed to go together. He mowed with a full sweep. He prided himself on being a four-acre mower; but that afternoon he could not put his heart into the mowing. The image of his wife leaning her head against the doorjamb kept coming before his eyes to trouble him.

3

She became suddenly shy of the idea of calling on the neighbors and after twice mentioning it, John let her alone. But next day, meeting Phelps, who had come over to mow his half of the swale, John thought it only polite to mention Delia's return. Phelps thought it was almost miraculous. He shook John's hand and vowed he would tell his women-folks that evening. John explained that Delia felt shy about meeting people. She had no decent clothes yet. Just the Indian things she had come home with. Phelps said he understood and they mowed all day without taking up the subject again.

But Mrs. Cutts was a curious woman and made a point of passing through Borst's clearing on her way home from the berry patch on Dygart's knoll. With no warning, Delia had no decent chance of getting out of her way and, when Mrs. Cutts asked if she could come in, smiled hesitantly and stood aside from the door.

"It's a good thing for John you've come back, Mrs. Borst," said the old woman, sitting down. "My, the sun's hot. But I got some dandy strawberries. I'll leave you some. I've got a real likin' for John." Her keen old eyes examined Delia frankly. "Phelps (I always called him Phelps, he used to be my hired man), Phelps said you was shy about your clothes. Land sakes! If I was a part as pretty in them I wouldn't be living with my son-in-law."

She smiled as Delia flushed.

"You ain't very talkative, are you?" she asked after a moment.

Delia got even pinker. "It's hard to be with people again — white people, I mean."

"It must have been hard," said Mrs. Cutts. "Did they burn everything you had?"

Delia nodded. "But I don't seem to mind it now. Not what happened to our place. We were lucky that way."

"Yes. John told me he was away. He said every other man but one and a boy got killed."

"That was the bad part, wondering what had happened to John." She walked over to the window. "I don't like to think about it, Mrs. Cutts."

"No wonder. Indians must be awful people. I expect they made a kind of slave out of you. They do that with their own woman, I've heard tell."

"Squaws don't think they're slaves. So they didn't treat me bad by their lights. You see I got adopted into a house."

Mrs. Cutts studied her shrewdly.

"You mean you was just like one of them?"

Delia nodded.

"I guess that's why you feel uneasy with white women. Listen, Mrs. Borst," she said, after a moment. "I don't know what happened to you out there. I don't want to know unless you want to tell me. I'm no gadder, if you want to. But I like John. You won't make him happy if you keep troubling yourself about what happened. It wasn't your fault, was it?" Delia shook her head. "You're healthy and pretty-looking, and you're still young. There's a long time ahead of you. It's not so easy for a woman to begin over as it is for a man, I don't know why. But you can do it if you want to."

Delia swung round on the old woman, who now had stooped to pick up her berries. "Give me a dish, dearie, and I'll fill it from my pail."

But Delia made no move to. She stared at Mrs. Cutts with painful intensity.

"What do you think happened to me, Mrs. Cutts?"

"I don't know. It's not my business and I'm not asking. Don't you worry. My tongue's my own and I keep it where it belongs." She gave Delia a hearty smile. "Now, where's a dish?"

She heaped the dish with the fresh berries and went out of the door. She was a dozen yards down the path before Delia thought of thanking her. She ran after the old woman, who by then had her shawl over her head and was stumping along like a vigorou; witch. Delia moved so quietly in her Indian moccasins that she startled Mrs. Cutts.

"I meant to thank you for the berries. They're lovely."

"You're real welcome to them," said Mrs. Cutts. "When you feel ready to, come over and see us. Bring John or come alone."

"Thank you. I'll walk along a way with you. It's time I went and told John to come to dinner."

"That's neighborly." Mrs. Cutts did not speak. She thought maybe the girl would unload her trouble. She knew she had one and the only way to get her to tell it was by keeping quiet.

But Delia walked also in silence. She was a good head

taller than Mrs. Cutts. Glancing sidewise, the old woman could see the thoughtfulness in her face. God, she thought to herself, studying the round of the chin, the straight nose and reserved eyes, and the large mouth, think of an Indian with that. They parted at the fork of the path without having said another word. Mrs. Cutts wasn't planning to say anything, but at the last moment she unexpectedly made up her mind.

"Delia Borst," she said. "Just remember that there's some things a man is a lot happier for not knowing. It may be hard on you; but it's true."

"The man might find out some time. Then what would he think?"

"I'd let him take his chance of it."

Delia looked over the top of Mrs. Cutts's bonnet.

"But I love John," she said.

4

She made up her mind to tell him that night. When he came in from the swale half an hour after her, he could tell that something was on her mind. She had been helping him all afternoon, raking his mowing of the day before into cocks. She seemed to take pleasure in the work and they kept at it all afternoon in companionable silence.

But she didn't say anything until she had given him his cornbread and broth, and then she came at it roundabout.

"Mrs. Cutts stopped in this morning, John. We had a talk."

"She's a neighborly woman," he said. "Though she's kind of short-spoken."

Delia got the dish of berries. "She left these for us. I didn't like her at first. But after a while I thought she was nice."

"She tell you about the way she broke her wrist?" Delia shook her head. "She will. She likes to talk about her troubles but she don't let them hinder her from doing what she wants."

"She didn't mention it. We got talking about what men think."

"Did you?"

"She said it was better for a man not to be told everything by his wife."

John said, "I guess that depends on the wife."

"That's what I said." She finished her berries and sat still, leaning slightly towards him over the table. She had the look of taking hold of herself with both hands. They were folded on the table edge, so that when she leaned against them they fitted the cleft in her breasts. Her hands could feel the beating of her heart.

"You look worried," John said suddenly.

But she did not notice him. Her eyes seemed lost in the darkness gathering beyond the open door. There was a fringe of balsams beyond the swale and their tips were like small arrowheads in the line of pale light still showing under a west-moving bank of clouds.

They had not lit the dip. Their only light was from the fire. An exploratory June bug buzzed through the door, flipped on one wing tip between them, and hit the stone back of the fireplace. Delia shivered and turned her eyes to her husband's.

"John, I've been home most a week, and you've never asked me what happened to me in Onondarha."

"Where was that?"

"That's the name of the town I lived in. You see, you never even asked me that."

John Borst also had become quiet. His big hands, which had been resting on the table, he put into his lap. She could imagine them holding his knees. His heavy face with its slow-moving eyes stared back at her. She drew her breath slowly, thinking how kind it looked. She had never heard his voice sound the way it did when he spoke to her.

"I didn't ask you because I figured you would tell me what you wanted I should know. What's all right with you is all right with me. I've wondered what happened to you sometimes. I got crazy about it sometimes. But now you're back I don't want you to tell me what you don't want to."

She was surprised and touched. "Mrs. Cutts almost said the same thing, John. Do you know what I said? I said I loved you too much. Maybe it's bad to love someone too much."

"Maybe," he said. It sounded stupid. He could see her trembling. The lift of her chin towards him was a hurtful thing to see; the complete quiet of her struggling with herself.

"I've got to tell you, John. You can send me away then if you want."

"I won't never send you away."

She put out her hand quickly as though to stop his lips, then let it fall to the table between them. "I won't take that for a promise," she said. "You've got to listen. I can't bear you loving me unless you know. High-Grass, the Indian that took me, got me adopted into his house. The women dressed me up and showed me how to make a cake and told me to give it to the old woman of the house. I didn't know what they said, I hadn't learned Indian then. You believe that?"

His voice sounded heavy. "Yes, I believe it."

"I didn't know I was getting married. I wanted to please them. I wanted to stay alive so I could come back to you. I didn't know till night when he came into my place. I didn't know it was his place till then. There were thirty people in that house all round me, John."

He didn't say anything. He didn't look at her. Her voice became more urgent.

"I couldn't do anything. Anything, John. I couldn't. I didn't think I could live."

"You did, though."

"Yes, I did." She sounded suddenly calmer. "After a year I had a baby, John. He was the only thing I loved. I didn't love him either. Every time I saw him I thought of you. I thought how you'd hate me."

"I don't hate you."

Her lips stayed parted. She licked them suddenly with her tongue, but even then she could not speak. After a while John got up. He turned to look out of the door.

"Where's the baby?"

"He died."

"You didn't leave him, did you?"

"No, John."

"That would have been a bad thing. Did you have any more children?"

"No." She whispered, leaning forward over the table. "I couldn't have come back, leaving a child, could I? And I couldn't come back with one. I thought when he died it was like Providence telling me I could come back. I knew I had to tell you. But when I got here, I couldn't, John. Honestly, I'm sorry."

He didn't notice her.

"This High-Grass," he said. "What's he doing?"

"He went off on a war party. He didn't come back. They told me he got killed."

"My God," he said. "I can't do nothing."

He turned through the door abruptly, leaving her at the table. She sat alone for a long time. She could hear him walking round. But she could not move. She waited like a prisoner until at last he came in. He said, "Ain't you done the dishes?" But she only shook her head and watched him. "Come on," he said, "I'll help you."

She rose slowly, reaching for the dishes blindly. "Do you want me to stay?"

He turned on her, his voice heavy with sarcasm.

"Where in hell could you go to this time of night?"

5

An outsider would have seen nothing unusual in their relations, and Delia herself was sometimes almost persuaded that John was putting what she had told him from his mind. But in a day or so she would catch him watching her; and at such times something in his eyes made her feel whipped and humiliated. She accepted the feeling as part of the payment she would have to make for what had happened to her — that she had known all along she would have to make. A good woman, she thought, a Christian saint, would have died first. But Delia hadn't wanted to die, she had wanted to get back to John; now she must take the future with patience.

It was hard to be patient living with John. Times were when she wanted to cry out, "Stop looking at me that way. I'd rather you'd whip me if you wanted. I didn't do anything bad." While they were working together in the field, it was more like old times, or hauling the hay up to the sheds in small loads on a sledge. The rick built slowly; but when it was high, John sometimes grinned pitching the hay up to her on top.

In the evenings was the time their reserve came between them. It arrived with the intimate darkness. She felt that he thought of her as just a useful body, something one accepted as one accepted the weather. But her resentment was less against him — she remembered how he had waited seven years for her and built the cabin where she expected it to be — than against the Providence that had played tricks with her. It got so she prayed that it might be reversed for even just one day.

One way he had changed was in laying down the law about their neighbors. He kept after her until she had made a dress from the calico he had brought. She could hardly bear to touch it, thinking of the impulse that had made him buy it at the very time of her return, and of what her return had resulted in. But he said he didn't want the neighbors to think he wasn't proud to show her off.

They made the visits one Sunday, she in the calico that felt like a cold rag touching her limply, he with his coat brushed. They went first to the Hartley house, to get the worst part over quick, John said.

Delia disliked them both. The man eyed her with open and curious admiration as if in his mind he lifted the hem of her skirt. The woman, in the one moment they had to be alone, asked, "Tell me, Mrs. Borst, are Indian men the same as other men?" "Why should I know?" Delia asked frigidly. Mrs. Hartley whinnied softly. "With the shape you've got. Oh my! Listen, I'd like to see you dressed in squaw's clothes. Phelps said you came back in them. Would you show them to me?" They were a strange couple to find in Dygartsbush, Delia thought; but she found the Phelpses nice simple people.

John was pleased at the way the Phelpses took to Delia and she to them. He wouldn't feel easy about leaving Delia alone when he went down to Fort Plain if she didn't have a place she could go to. Mrs. Cutts had said they'd be glad to have Delia visit them the next time he went down. The old woman had seen with one look that there was something between the Borsts; she guessed what had happened. She took John aside as they were leaving and said, "John, I want to tell you I think she's one of the best sort of women. You can see she's honest." Then she added, "When a person's young, he or she's likely to set a lot of store in notions that don't amount to much when they get older." She gave his shoulder a sharp pat and sent him after his wife before he could think of a reply.

He walked silently and morosely until he and Delia were near home. Then he asked, "Did you tell Mrs. Cutts anything about you and that Indian?"

As she turned her head to answer he could see that she was close to tears. "No. I didn't think anybody but you had any right to know."

"I think she must have guessed about you then," he said gloomily.

Thank God, he thought, Mrs. Cutts wasn't a talkative woman. She was smart, though, and she had probably guessed it. He couldn't hold it against Delia. He watched her getting their Sunday supper, and then got down his rifle to oil it. He would have to go down to Fort Plain again soon and he thought he might as well go that week. Anything to get out of the house. He glanced up to surprise her covertly studying him from the hearth. She turned her head at once, paling slightly. She made him think of an abused dog when she did that, and he felt a senseless and irrational burst of anger.

"What do you always want to be staring at me for?"

"I didn't mean to be staring at you. I didn't want to make you mad."

"I get sick of it."

She watched the fire. Then, "You hate me, don't you, John?"

"No. I don't hate you. But I can't stand that way you look." He got up suddenly to replace the gun. "Don't start talking that way, either."

"I can't talk at all, can I?" She turned on her knees to face him. "John, what sense is there in us living together like this?"

"Stop it. I'm going out. When you've got the supper ready I'll come in. I'm going to look at the heifer." It was a feeble excuse. He felt ashamed. The heifer wasn't due for a couple of weeks yet. He tramped down to the shed and looked her over. He stayed there fussing aimlessly about nothing until he heard Delia's tentative call. When he entered the house, she was sitting on her side of the table, and he felt an impulse to say something that would make her feel better.

"I guess I'll go down to Fort Plain tomorrow," he said. "I've got to get flour and I might as well go sooner as later. Maybe I'll hear something about my bounty land."

Neither of them believed he would hear.

"I'm sorry I talked that way," he said.

The corners of her mouth quivered.

"I know it's hard for you, John. It's hard for me. When you talk like that and look that way you make me feel like something dirty."

He relapsed sullenly into silence.

6

Though it was raining, he started next morning, letting the mare take her time so that they reached Fort Plain towards noon. He did his trading before dinnertime, finding that the price of salt beef had risen like everything else. Flour was pretty near prohibitive as far as he was concerned. Then he went round to Honus Kelly's to visit and ask whether there had been any news from Mr. Paris about his bounty land. Honus had gone out earlier that morning, he was told; no, no word had come for him from Mr. Paris. He might find Honus down at the tavern.

John didn't like to ask Honus's hired girl to give him food and she didn't offer him any, so he went down to the tavern in a gloomy state of mind. Nobody was in the place except the landlord and a couple of women in the kitchen. The landlord came into the tap and said he could give John some cold pork. John asked for some and ordered a strap.

The landlord said, "Quite some rain, ain't it?"

John said it was.

"I been looking in my almanac." The landlord fished out a worn book from under the bar, flipped the pages to August with a licked thumb, and said, "Look what the bug-tit wrote down about the weather." John looked at the column of "Various Phenomena" for August, but the landlord read out the words, "*Very hot. Hot and Dry.* Then he says *Cooler winds.* Way down at the bottom he's put in

Wandering thun. showers. I paid two and a half shilling for this book. Why hell, I could've wrote down that kind of stuff myself. And look at it rain and no *thun* (that's what he calls thunder) neither."

John said it didn't look very good to him and asked for Honus Kelly.

"He come in this morning," the tavernkeeper said casually. "He got Walrath, Pierce, and the two Devendorfs and they went off after an Indian that was in here."

John said, "That's too bad. I wanted to see him. Who was the Indian?"

A stout, red-cheeked woman brought in a plate of sliced fresh ham, bread, a cold roast potato with a slice of raw onion leaning against it. The landlord leaned over it as if to smell the onion. They looked desultory, like any two men in a taproom on a rainy afternoon. An investigating fly buzzed over from the window and the landlord slapped him down with the glass rag. Through the open door the sound of the eaves' drip from the low stoop continued steadily.

"Why, he acted all right when he come in here. Said he was heading south and asked about the settlements. I said there was some people living in Dygartsbush." The landlord looked up. "Why, that's where you're settled, ain't it? I forgot. You don't come down much."

John left off eating. His big face leaned intently towards the tavernkeeper's. "What was the matter with him?"

The tavernkeeper poured himself a drink.

"Makes my stomach turn to think of it. He got a couple of rums inside and commenced acting big. I told him to behave himself. I said we killed fresh Indians round here, but he just slammed his hand axe down on the bar and said he'd kill me if I didn't behave myself, the lousy old skunk. I didn't dast move out of the tap and there wasn't anybody else to send for Honus. So I just waited and pretty soon he got nervy and said he'd had enough and I told him what he owed me. Then you know what he did? He hauled out a kind of funny looking purse and I looked at it and said it was funny looking, and he held it out for me to look at. My Jesus, mister, it was the skin off a human hand. Looked to me like a woman's, honest to God."

The tavernkeeper looked into John's flushed face.

"Makes you feel ugly, don't it? He paid me in British money, too. I knowed then he was a genuine bad one. But by God I didn't tell him English money was worth twice York money. I made him pay straight, yes sir. He paid and went right through that door, putting that purse back in his coat pocket, and he clumb the fence and went into the woods. I tell you, I went right after Honus."

"How long was it before Honus got after him?"

" 'Bout an hour and a half. Honus has got the boys organized pretty well. I figure he'll pick him up before too long a time."

John spoke slowly, half to himself. "It's hard tracking in a rain like this one."

"Ain't it the truth? I hadn't thought of it. Still, Honus is good. Ain't any of these Indians has got away from him yet. The boys tell me about it, because they know I keep quiet. Tie 'em to trees, they say, don't hurt 'em at all. Only they use the neck-and-limb method."

The landlord had to laugh. Then he met John's eye and stopped short. "No offense, you know, mister."

John ignored him. "What did the Indian look like?"

"Why," he said. "Looked like any Indian. He had on an old hat and a coat, he'd probably stole. Looked pretty old — he'd let his hair grow and there was some white in it. But he was fat. I knew there was something about him. He had the biggest stomach you ever saw."

"Did he say what his name was?"

"Said he was Christian Indian. Christian boy, he said. Bet he was sixty years old. Called himself Joe Conjocky. Ever hear of him?"

John pulled out his purse. "What do I owe you?"

"My God, you've hardly et."

John picked up his rifle and started. But he stopped in the doorway, and the tavernkeeper thought his face was strangely set.

"Hey, you. Did you tell Honus how that Indian asked about Dygartsbush?"

"Why, no. Come to think of it, I guess I didn't."

"You damn fool."

John went out. He didn't run, but his big legs took him swiftly along the muddy road to the barn. He saddled his mare, packed on his flour and beef and salt, reprimed his rifle, and led her out of the barn. It was still raining.

The wind was southwest, bringing the rain against their faces, and the mare flicked the first drops from her ears. He swung up on her and headed her home. He had a sick feeling in his insides: twenty miles; a wet trail; and the

Indian had started at about ten o'clock. John figured it would be past one, now. Even if he pushed the mare hard enough to founder her, he could not expect to reach his cabin before suppertime. Delia would be coming back from Phelpses' long before that. He felt a sudden blaze of anger against the tavernkeeper. If the damned fool had only had the sense to tell Honus, Honus would have headed straight for Dygartsbush when the tracking got slow. But Honus wouldn't hurry. He'd follow his usual plan of getting up with the Indian about dark and taking him by his camp-fire. That was safe and easy, Honus said; and it saved a man the bother of lighting a fire for himself. The one sign of intelligence the fool tavernkeeper had shown was to recognize the Indian as a bad one. He couldn't help it though, after seeing that purse.

John wasn't an imaginative man, but he could guess how it had happened. A woman alone in her cabin, maybe with a child, you couldn't tell, and her man away for the day, hunting, or gone in to a settlement. The Indian, mousing into the clearing, quite openly, to beg some food, and find-ing out she was alone. Sitting himself down in the cabin. The woman scared half to death, getting his dinner. Him eating and watching her get more and more scared and cleaning his plate. Watching her clean up, waiting till she made a move to slip out.

The mare came to the first ford and nearly lost her foot-ing. John jerked her up and kicked her across. The creek had risen since morning. The rapids were frothy and begin-ning to show mud. The rain fell into the gorge without much wind, but John could see the trees swaying on the rim of the rock walls. The scud of cloud in the narrow belt of sky seemed to take the gorge in one jump.

The mare was a willing brute, but she had always been a fool about her feet. John settled himself grimly to ride her. He managed to keep her trotting a good part of the time, sitting well forward and squinting his eyes to look into the rain.

He had told Delia to stay at Phelpses' till he came home, but she wouldn't. She would start out in time to get home well before him. She said it was what a woman ought to do. A man ought not to come home from a long trip to have to wait for his food. She'd be there now, fixing the fire.

He seemed to see her kneeling in front of the fireplace, blowing the fire, pink-cheeked. And he could see the fat figure of the Indian trotting along through the woods for the clearing. Even a fat Indian could cover the ground; he'd have plenty of time to get there before dark. Delia wouldn't hear him. She wouldn't see anything either, not even his face in the window, because the panes were made of paper. She'd only hear the door squeak on its wood hinges; and even then she'd think it was John.

"God help her," John said, and the mare pricked her ears and he gave her a cut. He knew then that what had happened to Delia in the Indian country made no difference to him. It was what might happen to her before he could get home.

The ride became a nightmare for him. There was a lot of stony footing in the upper part of the creek section through which the mare had to take all the time she needed.

It was nearly dark in the gorge. The wet sky in the narrow opening was just a color overhead, without light. He got off and walked at the mare's head, and they came to the turn by the beech tree and climbed the steep ascent to the flat land side by side. The mare was blowing heavily.

John counted fifty to let her blow herself out, but she spent most of the time shaking herself. He swung onto her again and started her off at a trot.

On the high flats the woods thinned and now and then he got a canter out of her. They had more light, also, and in the west the clouds showed signs of breaking and he saw the sun once, nearly down, in a slit over the woods. Night came, however, when he was still three miles from home.

He thought he had made a mistake when he saw the light off the trail. For a minute it seemed to him that the mare must have done a lot better than he realized and that he had already reached Hartley's. Then he knew that the light was too close to the earth to come from Hartley's window. Someone was camping off the trail.

He cursed himself for not realizing it sooner and brought the mare up hard and tied her to a tree. To be sure, he picked out the priming of his rifle for the second time and reprimed. Then he slid into the underbrush and began working his way up to the fire.

He had not gone fifty yards before he saw that there were five men sitting round the fire and he recognized Honus Kelly's black beard. They were hunched close to the flames, with their backs to a brush lean-to they had set up, eating bologna and bread.

John got to his feet and started for them, shouting Kelly's name. He saw them stop laughing and pick up their guns and roll out of the firelight like a comical set of surprised hogs. When he got into the firelight he couldn't see any more of them than the muzzles of their guns.

"John Borst," roared Kelly, rising up. "What in the name of God are you doing here?"

"Where'd that Indian get to?" John asked.

"Oh, the Indian. How'd you know about him?"

"I've been down to Fort Plain. I heard about him in the tavern. The damn fool said he didn't tell you the Indian was asking about my place."

Honus let out a laugh. The others, who had resumed their places, left off picking the leaves from their bread to grin too.

"You didn't think he'd get away from us now, did you?" asked Honus. "The Indian's all right. He's just a piece above us."

He sat down, pointing his thumb over his shoulder. Looking upward, John saw moccasined legs hanging beside the bole of a maple. The fat body was like a flour sack, three parts full, inside the old coat.

Honus Kelly, watching John's face, said, "Sit down. You'd better."

But John shook his head. He could hardly speak for a minute. He was surprised because he still wanted to get home. But he tried to be polite.

He said at last, "You boys better come back with me. It's only a short piece and you can have a dry bed on the floor."

"No thanks," said Honus. "We got a good place here."
He saw that John was anxious to get on, so he rose to his
feet and put his hand on John's shoulder and walked back
with him towards the mare. "Delia and you won't be want-
ing a bunch like ourselves cluttering your place tonight,"
he said. Then he swore. "If Frank had told me about it,
I'd have sent a couple of boys straight up to you. We had
a time tracking him. It's been lucky all round."

John shook hands with him.

"You don't need to thank me," said Honus. "I always
wanted to get even with that Indian. Don't you remember
him? He used to hang out west of the settlement. Him and
me had trouble over my trap line once or twice."

He watched while John mounted. Then he caught hold
of the bridle to say, "We'll bury the rat. It's near the trail."
He looked up, his eyes showing white over his beard. "You
won't tell Delia?"

John shook his head.

"Best not," agreed Honus. "Well, good luck."

He slapped the mare's quarter and let her go.

7

It had stopped raining, but drops were still shaking off
the leaves. There were no stars. The woods smelled of the
rain, fresh and green. The air was light and felt clear
when he breathed it and the mare moved more perkily between his thighs. When she came into their clearing, John
saw a light in the cabin window. He saw it with a quick
uplifting of his heart, and he was glad now that Delia was

pigheaded about being home before him. He remembered how it used to be before her return, coming home alone, and fumbling his way in in the dark.

He rode by to put the mare in the shed and carried the load round to the door. It squeaked on its hinges as he pushed it open. Delia was kneeling by the fire, blowing it, her face flushed. She swung round easily. He had a quick recollection of the image he had made of the Indian entering. But her face wasn't afraid. It was only apologetic.

"I thought you weren't coming home, John. I let the fire go down. Then I heard the mare."

Her eyes were large and heavy from her effort to keep awake. He warmed himself before the sputtering fire, watching her struggle to get back her faculties. Suddenly she straightened up. "You're wet. You're hungry."

"I got delayed," he said. She went to the saddlebags, rummaging for food, and he said awkwardly, "I wanted to get some sausage but beef was so dear I didn't have money left for it."

"Oh John," she said, "I don't care." She started to heat water.

"There's a little tea though, and half a dozen loafs of sugar."

"White sugar?"

"Yes. You'd better have tea with me."

"I don't need it."

He felt embarrassed and shy. He didn't know how to tell her what he wanted to. He couldn't say, "I thought there was an Indian going to bust in on you and I got scared. But Honus hanged him, so it's all right." That wouldn't explain it to her at all. She was looking at him, too, in a queer, breathless, tentative way.

"You always used to like tea," he said. "You remember the first tea we had."

Her gaze was level, but her color had faded. Her voice became slow and her lips worked stiffly.

"You said, 'Will you have some tea?'"

John for a moment became articulate.

"No, I didn't say that."

"You did." The look in her face was suddenly pitiful. But he shook his head at her.

"I said, 'Will you have tea with me, Mrs. Borst?'"

She flushed brilliantly.

"Oh yes, John. And I said, 'I'd love to, Mr. Borst.'"

He needn't have worried about her understanding. It all passed between them, plain in their eyes. She didn't ask anything more.